JACQUES POULIN

Autumn Rounds

TRANSLATED FROM THE FRENCH BY

Sheila Fischman

archipelago books

Copyright © Jacques Poulin, 2002
Originally published as *La tournée d'automne* by Leméac Éditeur, 1993 Montréal
First published in English by Cormorant Books in 2003
English language translation © Sheila Fischman 2021

First Archipelago Books Edition, 2021

Library of Congress Cataloging-in-Publication Data
available upon request.

Archipelago Books
232 3rd Street #A111
Brooklyn, NY 11215
www.archipelagobooks.org

Distributed by Penguin Random House
www.penguinrandomhouse.com

Cover art: Jean Paul Lemieux
Interior design: Gopa & Ted2, Inc.

This book was made possible by the New York State Council on the Arts with the
support of Governor Andrew M. Cuomo and the New York State Legislature.
Funding for this book was provided by a grant from the Carl Lesnor Family Foundation.
Archipelago Books also gratefully acknowledges the generous support of the
Nimick Forbesway Foundation, Lannan Foundation, the Jan Michalski Foundation,
and the New York City Department of Cultural Affairs.

AUTUMN ROUNDS

THE BRASS BAND

H E OPENED the window so he could hear the music better. It was a marching tune played on brass instruments and drums. He leaned outside, but it was coming from the other end of the Terrasse Dufferin. The weather was fine so he decided to go out and have a look. He went down the five floors.

In the distance he saw a crowd in front of the Château Frontenac. He went up and joined them. The band consisted of a handful of musicians, along with jugglers, clowns, a woman singer and a black dog.

The singer was finishing her song. He couldn't help smiling: it was "La Java bleue." The crowd picked up the refrain. There was applause and the singer, who was wearing a long green dress with gold sequins, made a comical bow. Then the musicians put away their instruments and leaned against the guardrail of the Terrasse. He stood next to them so he could hear what they were saying.

They had come from France at the invitation of the Festival d'Été. It was their first visit to Quebec City. They'd probably been there for a few days already because they seemed very familiar with the broad bay that spread before them, with the south shore, the Beauport Hill, the Île d'Orléans nestled in the arms of the St. Lawrence River, and the mountains of Charlevoix far away on the horizon. They didn't hide their admiration of the expanse of this landscape.

From the corner of his eye he noted that the person leaning on the guardrail to his right was a woman. She had a white T-shirt and jeans of a blue that was neither too pale nor too dark – exactly the way he liked them.

She turned towards him.

"The view is magnificent!" she said warmly. Her voice was slightly husky.

"It is," he said.

"I thought that the Rhône was a great river but this one is much wider."

"Do you live in the Rhône valley?"

"Quite close. Near a small town called Tournon. Do you know it?"

He nodded. The woman came closer. She had curly grey hair and a bony face like Katharine Hepburn's. A beautiful face. A mixture of tenderness and strength.

"Are you with the band?" he asked.

"Yes," she replied, "but I'm not a musician. I handle bookings, reservations – all the practical details. I'm a little . . ."

"A little . . . everybody's mother?"

She smiled very sweetly.

"Do you like cats?" he asked abruptly. Then right away, he wished he hadn't asked, he waved his hand as if to tell her not to worry about it. He looked at her to see if her face had changed but no, she was still smiling.

"My name is Marie," she said.

He coughed to clear his throat.

"People call me the Driver. I have a van full of books – a book-mobile. My job is lending books."

"Do you have a regular route?"

"Yes. I visit the small villages between Quebec City and the North Shore. It's a big territory . . . I make one round in the spring, one in summer and one in the autumn."

He had trouble getting out the last word and his face darkened. The woman looked at him more closely. He turned his head, peered out at the misty horizon. They stood there in silence, side by side; they were the same height and they both had grey hair.

The members of the band moved away from the guardrail and gathered up their belongings.

"I have to go," said Marie. There's another show tonight. Will you come?"

"All right . . . I was late for the last one. I got here at the end."

"I know. I saw you."

"You did?"

She didn't answer. Her eyes were greyish blue and slightly mocking.

"It's at nine o'clock," she said. "Right near here, on the little square called . . ."

"Place d'Armes?"

"Yes. There are trees so we can set up the high wire. The name of the tightrope walker is Slim. At night it's really wonderful."

She left and joined the others.

It was five p.m. by the post office clock. He took a few steps in the direction of his place and then turned around, but the band had already disappeared. He bought an ice cream cone at the big stand on the Terrasse.

THE BLACK NOTEBOOK

To KILL SOME TIME, instead of going up to his apartment he walked to the end of rue Terrasse-Dufferin and into the narrow landway where the bookmobile was parked.

It was a two-tonne Ford delivery van. It was old and had done a lot of traveling, but didn't look its age. It was slate grey and it cut a fine figure with its curves, its window curtains and the word *Bookmobile* painted on the side in white.

He opened one of the rear doors, pulled down the step and climbed inside . . . After all this the magic still worked. the moment the door was shut you were in another world, silent and comforting, where the warmth of the books prevailed, with their secret scent, their many colors – sometimes bright and sometimes as sweet as honey.

The Driver was employed by the Ministry of Culture, which supplied the books. The bookmobile though belonged to him. It had originally been used to deliver milk and he had converted it with his father's help. Because there wasn't much room inside, the older man had got the idea of putting the shelves on tracks so they could be slid behind one another. The shelves sloped a little towards the back and they could be bolted in place. Behind them were a kitchen nook and a foldaway table and bed: the bookmobile was fitted out for camping.

He pushed open the curtain that masked the entrance to the cab.

Aside from the sand on the floor and the cats' paw prints on the windshield, everything was neat and tidy. He opened the glove compartment, took out the black notebook and went back to the library, where he sat on the floor in a corner. A few books were missing from the shelves, but it wasn't serious: the books were at the Ministry, in the bindery, and he had been assured that they'd be ready for the summer tour, which would begin in one week.

Another problem to solve: the new titles. The Ministry had sent him about twenty. They were at his apartment and he'd nearly finished reading them. Where was he going to put them? He was reluctant to give them the space occupied by old books. Even if they were only borrowed every now and then, in his eyes they were as important as the new releases. Besides, he mustn't forget that, new or old, the books were passed from hand to hand, and that was how the networks of readers had been formed.

For the fun of it he opened the black notebook and glanced at the different networks. There was now one in each of the areas where he stopped; most often it extended to several villages. In the notebook, each network was represented by a diagram, in which circles around the readers' names were connected by lines. It looked something like a molecular formula in a chemistry book.

The weather was hot and humid. He looked at the time and decided to take a nap. After sliding the shelving unit along its track, he opened out the bed and lay on his back, his head resting on the black notebook, his hands behind his head. He had wrinkles on his forehead and around his mouth, dark circles under his eyes and a hint of a smile on his lips.

THE ACROBAT

THE DRIVER took off his clothes on his way up the stairs. When he got to the fifth floor, bare-chested and holding one shoe, he ran into his neighbor, who gave him a bewildered look. Out of breath, he wished her a good evening, went inside and scattered his clothes over the three rooms of his apartment. He'd napped for too long and now he was late. Hungry too.

He put a pan of water on the stove to cook some pasta. Then he stepped into the shower. He emerged shortly after, hair dripping soapsuds, and tossed a handful of spaghetti into the boiling water. He noted the time, then got back in the shower. He rinsed his hair, then got out again to make sure that the saucepan wasn't boiling over. It wasn't, but just in case he plopped a lump of butter in the pot. Then went back to the shower to towel himself dry.

The pasta was ready before he had time to dress so he ate in his underwear, standing at the sink, with his fork in one hand and a hair-dryer in the other. Then he donned clean clothes and brushed his teeth. His watch read ten past nine when he raced down the stairs and headed for Place d'Armes.

The show had started.

The members of the band, wearing white shirts with blue stripes, were clustered in front of the fountain, surrounded by a fairly sizeable crowd. All eyes were on a man and a woman who were taking the black dog through a series of tricks. Not seeing Marie, the Driver tried to make his way through the spectators, but they were packed in too tightly. He decided to walk around the little square. When he spotted a place where the crowd was not so dense he slipped in and, by moving sideways, he was able to get close to the band.

All at once he spied Marie. She was in the front row of spectators, a few meters away ... She couldn't see him. With her face mirroring the emotions of the crowd, she looked even more beautiful than she had that afternoon.

At a nod from her, the jugglers came out. There were four of them. To the rhythm of the drums they began to juggle, some with balls, others with bowling pins, then they passed them back and forth, first two at a time, then all four together. They probably weren't the best jugglers in the world but they were clearly having as much fun as children; when they made mistakes they laughed at themselves. Now and then they would look over at Marie and they seemed to be juggling as much for her as for the audience.

After they had stopped, to warm applause, it was the singer's turn.

Her name was Mélodie. Accompanied by the musicians, she began to sing an old French song, "Mon pote le gitan." The Driver knew it well and murmured the words very softly:

My old gypsy pal is an odd-looking guy,
with his black-bearded face and eyes blue as the sky.

While she was singing in her warm, pure voice, Slim, the acrobat, had set up his wire between a tree and a metal post. Now he was sitting in the grass, quite still and abstracted. He wasn't dressed like the others: he wore an embroidered jacket and a scarf that gave him a bohemian look.

At a signal from Marie, there was a drum roll and Slim hoisted himself effortlessly over his wire. Silence fell over the crowd. Gazing at the horizon, the acrobat walked to the other end of the wire and on his way back, stopped halfway, flexed one knee and juggled some knives.

Just then the streetlamps on the Terrasse and on Place d'Armes came on and the scene became unreal and wonderful. The jugglers lit torches and tossed them to the acrobat on his wire and Slim spun against them in the air, tracing luminous circles that stood out against the darkening background of the canopy of heaven. Every so often streaks of life shone on Marie's face.

When the show was over, the Driver got in line with the people waiting their turn to toss a coin or a bill into the top hat that Marie had placed on the ground in front of the fountain. When his turn came he put a dollar in the hat, but she didn't see it: she was deep in conversation with Slim. He cleared his throat to get her attention but she didn't hear him, so he went away without speaking to her.

He was walking back to his apartment, head down beneath the streetlamps wrapped in mist that lined the Terrace, when on a sudden impulse he turned and ran back to Place d'Armes. Marie was still there. She was helping Slim put away his equipment. Hearing footsteps on the sidewalk, she looked up. He approached briskly, grasped her by the shoulders and rhymed off this sentence that he'd mentally rehearsed: "I just want to thank you for the emotions and the fantasy and the warm feelings." Then he kissed her on both cheeks.

His heart was pounding as he made his way home without turning around. But he'd still had time to see Marie's smile, a rather daunted smile. He took that image with him all the way to the buildings on rue Terrasse-Dufferin, to his small fifth-floor apartment and into his single bed.

A WRITER ON A CHAISE LONGUE

THE DRIVER very conscientiously read all the books the Ministry had sent him since the spring tour. Among the recent acquisitions was a novel by his friend Jack. He had enjoyed it very much, it was a good book, and he read the final chapters more slowly to postpone the moment when he'd have to take his leave of the characters.

But the book he had started reading that morning was a very serious study of communications within relationships; he was becoming seriously bored and the letters were swimming before his eyes. He decided to take a break and pay Jack a visit. His friend had his own distinctive way of seeing books.

Before he got behind the wheel he crouched down to see if there were any cats huddled under the truck. There weren't, but he never forgot to check because the bookmobile seemed to have retained a slight milky odor from its previous life that only cats could detect.

At the top of avenue Sainte-Geneviéve, he turned left onto Grande-Allée. Further along he took the Chemin Saint-Louis all the way to Cap-Rouge: it was there, on a cliff facing the St. Lawrence, that Jack and his wife Rachel lived, in a house not much bigger than a summer cottage. The old Volkswagen minibus, all rusted-out and falling apart, stood beside the house. The Driver parked the bookmobile behind the Volks, then he went to the back of the garden, near the tool shed.

Jack, wearing tennis shorts, was lying on a deck chair, a beer within easy reach on a metal table shaded by a parasol. He showed no surprise at the sight of the Driver, who often dropped in without warning. He didn't mind being caught while idle because he'd adopted a maxim of Philippe Dijan's: "Never lose sight of the fact that a writer lying on a chaise longue is, first and foremost, a man at work."

To tell the truth, Jack wasn't working at all. As usual, when he had just published a novel, he was incapable of beginning another until he'd started to hate the one he'd just published.

As he came closer, the Driver noticed that all the weekend papers were scattered around the writer's chaise longue and that his friend seemed rather blue. A good half-dozen empty cans were mixed in with the papers. Jack struggled out of the chair and shook his hand.

"How's everything?" he asked. "Rachel and I thought you'd left on your summer round."

"Not till next week," said the Driver. "What about you, how's it going?"

"Not great. Did you see the reviews? All favorable! Under those conditions, how am I supposed to hate my book? . . . It's a disaster!"

"Come on, it's not that bad!" said the Driver.

"Why d'you say that? . . . Have you seen anything negative? Anything unfavorable?"

"I'm fairly sure I did."

"You did? Show me!"

"In *Le Devoir*."

They rummaged among the papers, stumbling over empty beer cans, until the Driver found the books section of *Le Devoir*. He read aloud the first lines of the review of Jack's novel. "In book after book," wrote the reviewer, "he gives us the same character with the same character traits."

"See?" asked the Driver.

"No, I don't see a thing."

"Sure you do! He means that you're repeating yourself. That you can't bring anything new to your work."

Jack's face lit up.

"But . . . that's true!" he said. "You're absolutely right . . . I have to tell Rachel!"

He rushed to his house, calling his wife. Two minutes later the Driver saw him come back, looking very annoyed.

"She isn't there," he said. "I forgot: she's gone to Poste-de-la-Baleine."

Jack was an oddball. Writing took up so much space in his life that certain aspects of reality escaped him. For example, when his wife went on a trip he didn't realize it right away. Even though she'd left notes all over – on the kitchen table, inside the fridge, on the mirror of the medicine chest, in his *Petit Robert* dictionary. A lawyer and expert on Aboriginal matters, she often had to fly to the area around Hudson's Bay to defend the interests of the Cree or the Inuit whose lands were liable to be flooded by Hydro-Québec dams.

This time, she'd gone to Poste-de-la-Baleine to spend three days in a teepee with spruce branches covering the grounds.

"What will become of me?" Jack moaned. Without her, he was lost. He would forget to eat, he'd take sick, he'd come down with cancer.

"You've forgotten about the article in *Le Devoir*," said the Driver. "Now you'll be able to work."

"That's true. Thanks a million!"

"You're very welcome. By the way, I thought of something you could use . . ."

"What's that?"

"Something I read . . . A writer who doesn't like what people say about him in the papers decides to stop reading the articles and just count the number of lines the critic devotes to his book."

"Very good idea," said Jack. "I'll do that for the next one. It's high time I learned how to ignore other people's opinions and hate my books on my own."

Kneeling in the grass, he gathered up the papers and dropped them into a metal barrel where he burned leaves in the autumn.

"It's good of you to come," he said. "Would you like a drink? . . . Port? Vodka? White wine? Take a look in the kitchen cabinet, to the right of the sink . . . Make yourself at home."

The Driver went to the kitchen and opened the cupboard, but it was bare. Luckily, he found a can of beer in the fridge, the last one. When he returned to the garden, his friend was back in his chair, napping. He was smiling in his sleep. After looking up at the sky to check the course of the sun, the Driver arranged the parasol so that Jack's face would be in the shade as long as possible. Then he dropped a very gentle kiss on his friend's forehead, set the can of beer on the metal table and left the garden without a sound.

When Jack was preoccupied by his work he withdrew into himself and it was impossible to communicate with him. But there were a couple things the Driver would have liked to tell him. He'd have liked to tell him about the band, about the excitement at every street corner in the city, about Marie, who looked like Katharine Hepburn in *On Golden Pond*, and also about his next round in the bookmobile, which was going to be the last.

AN OLD WOODEN LADDER

As he was crossing the Jardin des Gouverneurs one morning, on his way to do errands, the Driver spotted the members of the band. They were sitting on the grass and talking with some municipal employees who were dismantling a temporary stage.

Timid as he was, he quickened his pace for fear that someone would recognize him. He left the park, walked down rue Haldimand, then stopped in the middle of the sidewalk. Just as he was hesitating between the grocery store on rue Des Jardins and the one on rue Saint-Louis, he saw Marie. She was carrying two bags of groceries that must have been heavy because she was holding them against her chest, with her hands joined over them.

"Good morning, Marie," he said. He couldn't help it, his voice was a little quavery.

"Morning," she replied.

In the harsh, nearly cutting light of late morning her face seemed more angular but as beautiful as ever, and her grey-blue eyes were still sparkling.

"Are those bags heavy?" he asked.

"Not really. . . We're having a picnic in the park; would you like to join us?"

"I wouldn't be in the way?"

"Absolutely not."

"May I?" he asked. He took one of her bags. She didn't object and they continued up rue Haldimand.

Bottles clinked in the Driver's bag.

"It's wine from France and beer from Quebec," she said.

"What's in yours?" he asked.

"Sandwiches and little cakes."

"I'm very glad to see you."

"Me too."

They walked slowly. The hill was steep.

"Will you be going back to France now that the festival's over?"

"Not right away. We want to travel around Quebec for a while . . . maybe see part of the States too. And something's come . . ."

"Is something wrong?"

"No," she said, smiling. "We've got a job playing jazz at the Clarendon for a few days. They'll lend us whatever instruments we don't have."

The Clarendon was the hotel where the band was staying.

"That's great!" said the Driver.

"Mélodie's very good at singing the blues. Will you come and hear her?"

"Will . . . will you be there?"

"Yes," she said and they fell silent. They were now back at the park. The musicians teased Marie about how long it had taken her to go to the grocery store and about the fact that she hadn't come back alone. In the midst of their laughter, Marie made the introductions and the *déjeuner sur l'herbe* got under way.

The Driver sat off to one side, leaning against a big oak tree. He drank a glass of wine so he'd be more comfortable with the others, but it was obvious that his restrained manner didn't bother them. They left him alone and laughed a lot among themselves. The black dog ran from one to another in search of a piece of sandwich. Marie talked to everyone. When she came to sit beside him he asked:

"Do you all live together near Tournon? . . . I mean, do you all live in the same area?"

"I live with Slim," she said. "He's my boyfriend . . . Mélodie, the singer, lives next door but she's often at our place. The others live in the hills or on the Rhône."

"Ah, so it's a hilly region . . ."

"There are hills everywhere. They go in every direction, the light changes constantly and the countryside is very gentle. Besides that, we see all kinds of birds."

"What's the house like?"

She picked up a sandwich and gave him half, then she began to describe the place. It was an old stone house that had its back to the road and opened onto a big inner courtyard; on one side of the courtyard was a low wall overgrown with shrubs and flowers and on the other side, a two-storey shed of which the top part was lined with straw and inhabited by a family of cats.

The Driver sometimes came to a kind of secret understanding with people who liked cats, one that went directly to the essential; it was as if they had known each other forever.

"How do the cats get down to the courtyard?" he asked.

"There's an old wooden ladder," said Marie. "They go down the ladder."

"And the kittens?"

"The mother picks them up in her mouth. Can you picture it?"

"Wait a minute . . ."

He closed his eyes, resting his head against the old oak tree. An amused smile drifted across his face while Marie described how the mother cat would go down the ladder holding a kitten by the scruff of the neck and set it down in the grass with a strange cooing sound, then hurry back up for one more and then another, until all the kittens were together in the sun-drenched courtyard.

Opening his eyes, he saw that Marie had moved a few feet away from him. She and her friends were gathering up the papers and the remains of the picnic to put in the trash. She came back and sat next to him.

"Are you all right?" she asked softly.

"I'm fine," he said. "Was I asleep for long?"

"Not really . . . Finish your sandwich, we're in no hurry."

"Are you going somewhere?"

"We're going for a walk in the neighborhood. Can you suggest a place?"

He thought it over as he ate his sandwich. It was a beautiful day, less oppressive than it had been, so he suggested they walk along the walls of Old Quebec. And as it wasn't easy to describe the route without a map, he offered to be their guide.

Taking the lead with Marie, he led them to rue Sainte-Anne at the end of which they climbed onto the walls, scrambling up the embankment at the Porte Kent. At the top, they turned onto a grassy path and kept moving, because of the strong smell of manure from the *calèches* parked on the Esplanade. A little further along they sat in the wild grass growing along the wall. The Parliament was across from them and on the right, they had a wonderful view of the Laurentians. Leaning over to Marie, the Driver recited:

As she walks past the old tennis courts of the parliament buildings, the sight of the distant mountains and sky briefly, surprisingly, touches her heart.

"Who said that?" she asked.

"Anne Hébert, in *The First Garden* . . . Right here, when I was little, there was a tennis court, a really beautiful one, and we'd come and sit on the wall to watch the matches. I remember, sometimes I couldn't resist looking up during the game and then the mountains were so beautiful, it was nearly painful."

"I understand."

They took the time to admire the gentle outline of the mountains that heralded the grand northern landscapes, then Marie began to talk about the places the musicians wanted to visit. The people they'd spoken to here and there always mentioned the same areas: Charlevoix, the North Shore, the Gaspé Peninsula.

"Would you mind if we came part of the way with you?" she asked.

"Not at all," he said. "But how will you get around? The bookmobile's really too small . . ."

"I know," she said, laughing. "We thought we might be able to buy a truck or an old bus. We've done that in Europe."

"You'd need something fairly big. An old school bus, something like that. If you want I can try to find you one."

"Would you do that?"

"Of course."

She leaned over to him. He held his breath while she kissed him on the cheek. Then they got back on the path and tried to catch up with the others, who had continued walking along the wall in the direction of the Porte Saint-Louis. They caught up on the other side of the gate, where the group had stopped at the edge of the slope that went down to the Plains of Abraham; they were watching the comings and goings of a family of groundhogs.

Turning his back to the vast green undulating park with its flowerbeds and clumps of trees, the Driver took them to the Citadelle. Behind it, they crossed a footbridge over the access road to the fortifications, then turned onto an asphalt pathway that went around the old fort and led to the edge of Cap Diamant.

There, they came to a standstill; the majesty of the St. Lawrence River took their breath away. They who joked and fooled around on the slightest pretext stood there for a good while without a word, stunned and wide-eyed. Then they slowly started down a broad wooden staircase that would bring them to the Terrasse Dufferin. The staircase was held up by girders that leaned against the rocky cliff and the low wall of the Citadelle; at each level, there were lookouts where walkers could rest.

As they made their way down towards the Terrasse, the landscape widened before their eyes. Leaning on the handrail at a lookout, Marie pointed at the Île d'Orléans:

"I'd love to go to that island," she said. "Is it beautiful?"

The Driver nodded. "Very beautiful," he said.

"Is that where Félix Leclerc lived?"

"Yes," he said, lowering his voice.

"Mélodie likes to sing 'le P'tit Bonheur' with the band."

Two musicians walking by began to hum Félix's song, which was then picked up by those coming behind, all the way to the highwire artist and the singer at the end of the procession.

"Still," said Marie, "it's not my favorite song."

"It isn't?"

"No. The one I like best . . . I can't remember the title but maybe I could sing it to you."

She collected her thoughts for a moment, then began to sing in her strange little voice:

> *I ache at your side*
> *You ache in my eyes*
> *That's true, it's false, it's both*
> *And this little bouquet*
>
> *So fresh in your hand*
> *Tomorrow will feed the soil*
> *And that's the truth*

She sang a few more verses and the Driver made an effort to sing along but the words stuck in his throat.

A STREAM AND SOME LITTLE RABBITS

IN THE CLARENDON BAR, the Driver got in the habit of sitting at the same table in a corner. First he'd check to see if Marie was there, then he'd order something light – a glass of wine, a beer, sometimes a hot chocolate, sipping it slowly as he listened to Mélodie and the band.

In this small dark room, where the ceiling fans weren't able to drive away the blue cigarette smoke, Mélodie was a different person; here, she didn't try to make people laugh. It was moving to see how much sincerity she put into her interpretations of the blues, especially songs from the repertoire of Ella Fitzgerald and Billie Holiday. If it weren't for her accent, you'd have thought that she'd been born in the Deep South.

Her greatest hit was Billie Holiday's song "Don't Explain." She sang it accompanied very softly by piano, sax, and double bass. It was the story of a woman whose husband came home very late at night; she told him that she'd seen lipstick on him, that she'd smelled a new perfume, that it was easy to guess the rest. She didn't ask him for an explanation, though: all she wanted was that he wouldn't leave.

There was another song that the Driver liked a lot: Leonard Cohen's "Famous Blue Raincoat."

When she sang it, Mélodie dressed like a man and assumed a deep voice, a monotone that was at the same time rich with shading. This song was about a man who was writing a letter to the person who'd taken his woman. Calling him "my brother, my killer," he told the man that it was four in the morning, that New York was cold, that the woman was nobody's wife; and he thanked him for taking the trouble from her eyes, which he'd thought was there for good.

Slim, the acrobat, accompanied Mélodie on guitar when she sang that rather strange song.

Most often, the Driver wasn't alone at this table. Marie would sit with him and between two songs they'd talk about the song and the books they knew. Like all shy people, the Driver had some idiosyncratic ideas: for instance, he was convinced that if two people were really made to get along together, they should like not only the same books and the same songs, but also the same passages in these books and songs.

Sometimes his friend Jack would join them, and sometimes his sister Julie, who lived in Beauport, across the bridge from the Île d'Orléans.

Julie was a teacher and the mother of two boys; she had a very nice husband who didn't mind looking after the children. The Driver felt a special attention for his young sister. He'd played hockey, tennis, and baseball with her; she was sturdily built and he had to be careful when he put his arms around her for a laugh, because she'd taken a course in self defense and was quite capable of landing him on the floor. Yet it took nothing – she might brush him with her elbow as she went by, or toss back her hair with a movement of her head, or pull up the hem of her skirt to show him where her cat had scratched her – to make him crazy about her and want to hold her in his arms.

Before she got married, she'd suffered terribly from a broken heart and he had taken her in. She had been depressed and had behaved like a child, so he'd washed her and fed her and rocked her and consoled her.

One evening, the Driver was alone with Marie. Mélodie had put a lot of soul into her performance and they were both moved. They didn't feel like talking.

At the break, the stage lights went out, the house lights came back on and the musicians went out the door onto rue Des Jardins to get some fresh air.

Marie got up. "Excuse me," she said, "There's something I have to tell Slim."

"That's all right," said the Driver. He looked at his watch. "I think I'll go home now," he added.

"No, stay a while. I just want to know where they're going after the show. If they want to spend all night in the bars on Grande-Allée, I'd rather rest or go for a quiet walk in town."

"All right, I'll stay. But first, can I ask you something?"

"Yes."

"Do you like Boris Vian?"

"A lot. Was it the blues that made you think of him?"

"Of course. Which of his books do you like best?"

"L'Écume des jours," she said. "Why?"

The waiter came over to take their orders.

"There's one sentence in it that I like a lot," said the Driver. "A short one around page forty or a little later. Colin is talking about Chloé's perfume and then he says something to a girl . . ."

"Oh, yes, I remember," said Marie.

She sat down again and asked the waiter for a pen and a piece of paper from his order pad. On the back of the paper she wrote: "It's wonderful! . . . You smell of the forest, with a stream and some little rabbits." She held out the paper. The Driver read what she'd written and his face lit up, then he folded the paper in two and put it in his shirt pocket.

"Can I get you anything?" asked the waiter.

"A coffee," she said.

"Same here," he said, looking into Marie's eyes.

"Okay," said the waiter, "two coffees."

THE SLEEPING ISLAND

H E COULDN'T SLEEP.
His pillow was damp. It was hot and very humid again. Though the bedroom and kitchen windows were wide open, there wasn't a breath of air. He switched on the bedside light and looked at his alarm clock: three a.m.

He closed his eyes and tried to get to sleep. He was calm. He had no reason to worry because everything was ready for the summer tour. Never had he prepared so carefully for a tour.

The truck's motor had been tuned up, the brakes checked, and the system of shelves on tracks had been inspected; despite its age the bookmobile was in good shape.

The Driver had finished reading the new books, both adult and children's, and he'd managed to find room for them on the shelves. That meant he didn't have to transport them in boxes that he'd have had to stow in the cab, behind the seats. The space was already taken up by two rather massive wooden chests: one contained all the tools for the truck, the other, manuscripts turned down by publishers, whose authors had entrusted them to the bookmobile in the hope of finding some readers anyway – which did happen now and then.

He had shipped three boxes of books to the municipal library in Baie-Comeu, the town he would reach mid-tour, and once he was there, he would collect them to restock his shelves.

Finally, he had gone over in detail the networks of readers recorded in his black notebook. Yes, everything really was ready. He was waiting to leave until the people in the band were well along in the repair and outfitting of the school bus he'd found for them; they were cleaning it now and getting it back in working order.

The Ministry left it up to him to decide when to set out. Over the years they had shown more and more confidence in this rather eccentric driver who combined the diligence of a civil servant with the capriciousness of a nomad.

He still couldn't get to sleep. He got up and leaned out the bedroom window. There must have been fog on the river because the lights of Lévis, reflected in the water, were blinking faintly. He liked fog so he got dressed, tossed a sweater over his shoulders and went downstairs to walk on the Terrasse-Dufferin. Even though it was the middle of the night there were people out, strolling or prowling. He took a few steps to the right, to the foot of the long wooden staircase, but there were couples embracing in the half-light under the last kiosk. To avoid disturbing them he made his way to the other side, walking close to the railing; he didn't want to lose sight of the lights that were dancing in the dark water, following the swell stirred up by the ferries and the freighters.

Ahead of him the Château Frontenac, lit up in green and gold, seemed like a legendary giant keeping watch over the sleeping houses nearby. Close to the funicular that led to the Lower Town, in the light of a streetlamp, he suddenly spied a silhouette leaning against the guardrail. Despite the distance, he recognized Marie. She was looking toward the Île d'Orléans. So as not to frighten her he coughed several times, then he took a few steps into the light and stopped.

"Bonsoir!" he said.

She turned her head in his direction.

"Bonsoir!" she replied in her husky voice. She bent her head and her grey hair shone in the light of the streetlamp. The Driver came up to her and kissed her cheeks, a little too high up, on the cheekbones that he liked so much. Then both of them, ill at ease, turned to face the river.

"I was hoping I'd see you," he said, "but I wasn't sure."

"Couldn't you sleep?" she asked.

"No. You?"

"Me neither. It must be the coffee."

"What about the others?" he asked.

"They're in a bar on the Grande-Allée."

"Are you cold?"

"A little. It's the humidity . . ."

"Would you like my sweater?"

"That would be nice."

It was his old grey sweatshirt with the hood. It was mended all over, you'd have thought it had gone through both world wars, but the Driver was very attached to it. He put it over Marie's shoulders and, turning her so that she was facing him, he tied the sleeves under her chin. All this he did so gently that a passerby might have thought that he was taking her in his arms.

"Thank you," said Marie. Then she pointed to the Île d'Orléans, wrapped in fog. "How do you get there?" she asked.

"Where?" he asked.

"To the island. Do you take the bridge over there that's all lit up?"

She pointed to a string of lights sparkling in the fog to her left, but it was the Dufferin Highway. The Driver took her arm and moved it slightly to the right.

"The bridge is just over there," he said. "It's hard to see with the fog."

"And is it very far from here?"

"No, fifteen minutes by car. Or by bookmobile . . . Would you like to go there!"

"I'd love to, but maybe you'd rather sleep."

"Not at all!" he protested. The determined sound of his voice showed clearly that for him, the thought of driving around the Île d'Orléans at three a.m. was the most natural thing in the world.

She linked arms with him and they crossed the Terrasse again to get to the laneway where the bookmobile was parked. The Driver didn't have the key so he used the one he kept hidden under the fender for emergencies. After he'd opened the passenger door to let Marie in, he took a flashlight from the glove compartment, knelt down and shone the light under the truck. He just had time to see a white ball of fur with two phosphorescent eyes run away: it was Blanca, the neighbor's little cat.

"Would you like to drive?" he asked.

"No," said Marie. "But thanks for offering."

He backed out of the parking space and drove up avenue Sainte-Geneviève and through Old Quebec, where there were still a good number of revelers even though the festival was over. Across from the Parliament building he turned onto the Dufferin Highway, and the bookmobile glided towards the Lower Town in a long lazy turn that brought it from the bridge to the island. Marie thought that the curved line of streetlamps bending over the road showed solicitude. Now and then she turned to look at the lights of the city, particularly those of the Château, the Prince Building, and the Parliament, which receded slowly into the foggy night. Soon they were at the bridge.

"It's very elegant, very harmonious," she said. Then she realized that he was smiling. "What are you thinking about?" she asked.

"Nothing," he said, "but you use the same words I do."

They climbed up a steep hill and at the top, the Driver hesitated. "We can circle the island from the right or the left," he said.

"And I have to decide?"

"Yes, please."

"Okay – let's go to the right."

He did so, accelerating smoothly to avoid making noise. All was calm; there was no one on the road and the village of Sainte-Pétronville was deserted. At the tip of the island a light wind came up, dispersing the fog, so they stopped on the wharf near a hotel to gaze at the lights of Quebec City. The moon was full and as red as glowing embers.

When they got back on the quiet, winding road, Marie took a moment to study their route on a road map she'd found in the glove compartment. At the village of Saint-Laurent the old houses, the chalets at the water's edge, the old tennis court – all were sleeping. On the other side of Saint-Jean, she noticed a motionless light on the river and he told her it was Île Madame. When they left Saint-François, the road turned left in front of the church. A little further along, the Driver stopped at a service area so they could stretch their legs. On grounds lit only by the moon, they spotted toilets, picnic tables, and at the very back, a big wooden observation tower.

"What can you see from the top of the tower?" Marie asked.

"In the daytime," he said, "you can see the headland very clearly and some of the small islands. At night, though, I have no idea . . ."

"Shall we go up and see?"

"If you want."

He took the flashlight and a blanket from the bookmobile and they set out to climb the rough wooden steps; they stopped at each landing to catch their breath and to see how the view had opened up.

At the top, he doused the flashlight. The air was cooler, the wind stronger, so he draped the blanket around Marie's shoulders over the old grey sweatshirt, and then around his own. When they turned toward the headland they couldn't make out the small islands, only the river that shone in the light of the red moon, along with the lights on either shore; he showed her those of Beauport where his younger sister lived. In the distance, to the southwest, the lights of Quebec City and Lévis merged.

"Marie . . ." began the Driver.

"Yes?" she said.

"I feel really good with you. That hasn't happened to me for ages."

"Same here."

"But I have to tell you something and it's a bit difficult."

Under the blanket she took his hand. He looked out ahead of him and declared firmly: "Getting old is something that doesn't interest me in the least. I decided a while ago that the summer tour would be the last. Do you understand?"

She squeezed his hand gently to tell him that she did or that she'd try to. They stood there silently, neither of them wanting to say anything more. Then, realizing, that she was shivering, he suggested:

"Shall we have a hot chocolate in the van?"

"All right," she said.

Accustomed now to the half-dark, they came down without using the flashlight. At the last landing, Marie stopped abruptly.

"I see an owl."

"Where?"

"Just at the edge of the woods, on a fence post."

She pointed, but the Driver couldn't see it.

"It's a medium horned owl," she pointed out.

"I can't see a thing," he said a little sadly.

Inside the bookmobile he slid the shelves aside and put water on the hotplate to boil. Above the sink was a photo that was always with him, protected by a plastic sleeve. It showed the Paris bookstore Shakespeare and Company. The photo had been taken at dusk and a bright golden light came from the store windows and spread into the bluish shadows.

Before long the heat under the kettle had warmed them, but neither one felt like talking. They drank the hot chocolate in silence and nibbled some maple cookies. Soon a grey light crept through the rear windows of the van and they hurried back up the tower to look towards the East. Wrapped in the blanket, huddled close to one another, they formed a single person: they looked like a sailor perched in the crow's nest of an enormous ship.

As they waited for the sun to appear, Marie turned towards the Driver. She pressed her cheek against his and in a very gentle and sisterly way, began to rub the cheekbone he loved against his eyes and the corner of his mouth.

THE FIRST TIME

T HE DRIVER set out on his summer rounds one morning around
ten o'clock, with the musicians in their school bus following
close behind. It was already unbearably hot and they were all glad
to be heading north. As they were about to leave, Marie decided to
ride with him part of the way.

In the mountains of Charlevoix, he kept glancing in the rearview
mirror and slowing down so he wouldn't get too far ahead of the old
bus, which was having a hard time on the hills. Marie was worried.
Would the brakes on the school bus hold out during steep drops?
What if the musicians who'd repaired them had overlooked some
detail?

When they came in sight of the breathtaking descent toward Baie-
Saint-Paul, Marie felt she had to have a word with Slim.

"Can you stop somewhere?" she asked.

"Sure," he said.

Immediately he switched on his turn signal. He made sure that the driver of the bus behind him was doing the same, then swung into a restaurant parking lot at the top of the hill. A few moments later the bus pulled up alongside the van. Slim was driving.

Marie got out to talk to her friend, who stayed in the bus with his head bent down toward her. The others leaned out of the windows to admire the little town, nestled in a vast semicircle of greenery, and the Île aux Coudres, which faded away in the light mist rising off the river.

The Driver was also looking at the landscape. His eyes were wet when Marie came back to sit beside him.

"You have mist in your eyes," she said very softly.

"Just a little," he said. "It's nothing."

"It's as if certain landscapes are . . . they're part of us and we can't be separated from them, don't you think?"

Amazed that she had guessed what was going on inside him, he didn't know what to say in reply and they both were silent. Then she talked about the brakes on the school bus.

"They seem to be working all right," she said. "We can go now."

He started up again, taking time for one last look at the landscape, then began their descent. The school bus followed not far behind them. At the foot of the hill they made a tight right turn that brought them to the center of town, and Marie turned around to see how the old bus was doing the curve.

"They're fine," she said.

She and Slim had agreed that it would be wise to stop at the first chance they got to check the brakes again, and maybe the steering and suspension too. She asked: "When you're working, is Baie-Saint-Paul one of your usual stops?"

"No," he said, "I only stop in the small villages. I mustn't compete with the libraries and bookstores."

"Of course not."

"But I don't have a precise timetable, so if you'd rather . . ."

He fell silent. Just ahead of them a little chipmunk was crossing the road along a hydro wire strung between two poles.

"Yes," she said, "I'd rather you went there, if that's what you were wondering."

Her husky voice was very gentle. To conceal his emotions he began to explain how they could organize their stay in Baie-Saint-Paul. If they wanted comfort they could go to a campground on the shore of the Riviére du Gouffre; if they chose to be more economical, they could simply park in some public place.

Marie preferred the second choice.

"We don't have much money," she said. "Soon we'll have to put on shows so we can pay for our gas."

"Then the best thing would be to park next to the church. We're nearly there."

A kilometer later he drove off the main road and turned left onto the grounds of the church. He let the school bus pass, gesturing to Slim that he should park on the right, where the shadow of the church would lengthen over the course of the afternoon. It was half-past twelve and the fog was thinning out under a slight breeze from the west. Marie said goodbye, brushing against his arm, and got out to help Slim park. The Driver put the van on the same side as the bus, but at the edge of the churchyard.

He had lunch by himself, without worrying about the others, his two back doors open because of the heat. Then he took a nap, after putting in earplugs to muffle the sounds of voices and tools . . .

In his dream a woman was outside looking at him, twenty paces from the van. He opened his eyes and propped himself on one elbow: she was still there. He waved and gave her a sleepy smile.

Sitting up, he realized all at once that it wasn't Marie. It was a very old woman. A little old lady.

Briskly he got up, folded the bed into the wall and replaced the shelf unit, sliding it along its track. Then he got out of the van.

"Bonjour, Madame," he said.

"Bonjour."

She took a few steps and stopped. She was all shrunken and tottery. In spite of the heat she was wearing a black dress buttoned to the neck, black stockings and a hat of the same color, with a little veil that didn't really hide her wrinkled face.

To encourage her he asked: "Would you like a book?"

"If it's no trouble, Monsieur."

"On the contrary, I'd be delighted," he said. Even when he wasn't working he made it a point of honor never to refuse anyone a book.

The little old lady walked up to the back step.

"This is my first time," she said. She took a spotless handkerchief from her sleeve and dabbed at the corners of her mouth.

"I understand," he said, and approached to help her into the bookmobile. Just then she lifted her veil and he saw that she had green eyes, amazing eyes that seemed to have a special gift for capturing the light.

"I saw what's written on the side of the van," she explained.

"I was just leaving the presbytery . . . The others, over there, what do they do?"

"They're performers. Musicians and jugglers."

She nodded. "What kind of books have you got?" she asked.

"All kinds," he said. "Would you like to come in and take a look?"

He held out his arm. She leaned on him as she climbed onto the step. Inside, he showed her how the books were arranged and where the various sections were. Then he left her alone; he got out of the van and took a stroll, but not too far.

At the school bus, the brake-check was over and calm was restored; oily newspapers had been left near the rear wheels. All the band members were inside, except for one musician who was practicing juggling with three tennis balls. Someone was hanging curtains at the windows, so the Driver couldn't see what Marie was doing.

As he walked, he watched the old lady from the corner of his eye. She was studying the books one by one, but didn't pick them up. With her head cocked to one side, she was content to read the titles; now and then she would stroke a spine with the tips of her thin fingers. He came closer and, hearing her sigh, he sat on the step.

"Is something wrong?" he asked.

"I can't," she said feebly.

"You can't?"

"There are too many books."

"That's true. I'll help you choose. But first, would you like a drink? Some lemonade?"

"Why yes, I'd like that. I can see that you've been well brought-up."

"Thank you!"

He climbed into the truck and offered her a folding chair. Opening the kitchen nook, he took the lemonade from the fridge and poured her a glass. She thanked him. He poured half a glass for himself, then replaced the shelf unit and took a seat on a stool.

"Have you lived in Baie-Saint-Paul a long time?" he asked.

"I was born here," said the old lady, taking a sip. "I've always lived here except for my year at school."

"You were a teacher?"

"Yes, I replaced a schoolmistress who was sick. That was in a small village in the mountains — Saint-Ferréol-les-Neiges. Do you know it?"

She waved her hand toward the Southwest and her movement, like the fearful expression on her face, suggested that the village was at the end of the world.

"Yes, I do," he said.

He asked some more questions and bit by bit the old lady described a school on a concession road where she had lived full-time, teaching pupils in several grades, all in a single classroom, grouped around a wood stove; she recalled the smell of woolen mitts and tuques and scarves drying by the stove in winter.

When she'd finished her reminiscences and her lemonade, the Driver got up and, without hesitating, took a book from a shelf.

"Here's one that might suit you," he said.

"Oh yes?" she asked, her eyes bright.

She held out her hand and he gave her a book by Gabrielle Roy, entitled *Children of My Heart*. It wasn't the paperback edition but an older one, with larger type that would be easy for her to read.

"Thank you," said the old woman. "Thank you very much."

"You're more than welcome," he said, and added that there was no form to fill out. She just had to mail the book back to the address printed inside the cover. If she felt like it, she was allowed, even encouraged, to lend it to other people.

Obviously pleased with these instructions, she thanked him again.

Then she struggled out of her chair and he helped her out of the van. She smiled timidly, lowered her veil and walked away down the main street, holding the book by Gabrielle Roy against her chest.

He had noticed the luminous quality of her eyes again as she was lowering her veil. She must have been very beautiful at one time. On the mantelpiece in her house there must be an old photo in a brass frame of herself as a young bride.

THE CAT ON ÎLE AUX COUDRES

T HAT MORNING as he was pouring cornflakes into his bowl, he heard a gentle tapping at the back of the bookmobile.

"Just a minute!" he said. Looking into the rearview mirror in the cab, he combed his hair with his fingers, then went to open the door. It was Marie. The lovely Marie with her grey hair and her smile and the quiet strength that radiated from her.

"Bonjour," he said. "How are you?"

"Fine," she said.

"Did you sleep?"

"A little. You?"

"Yes. Just before dawn."

Some of the musicians had spent the previous evening in town and they'd got together with a small orchestra that was playing in a restaurant. At closing time, the band members had gone with them to the school bus and they'd all played music together, drinking beer and wine. Despite his shyness, the Driver had joined them. They'd all gone to bed very late.

Marie's eyes looked smaller than usual.

"Aren't you coming in?" he asked.

"No," she said. "I just came to ask you something."

"How about some coffee?"

"Well . . . all right! Thanks a lot."

She climbed inside, leaving one of the two doors open. He switched on the hotplate to boil water. When the coffee was ready he poured a cup for Marie, who was sitting on the floor with her back against the sloping library shelves. Then he put milk in his cornflakes, folded up the table and chairs and sat down across from her.

"My head's still full of music," he said.

"Mine too," she said, taking a sip. "Mmm . . . this coffee's very good!"

"Thank you."

"You got to bed late because of us . . ."

"It doesn't matter," he said.

"Besides that," she said, "I've got a favor to ask you."

Unhurriedly, he ate his cornflakes and waited for her to explain.

She hesitated and he smiled to encourage her. Finally, she took the plunge:

"I'd really like to see the Île aux Coudres . . . Would you mind very much taking me there? And also Mélodie and Slim. The others would rather sleep or write letters or hang around in town and they . . ."

"I wouldn't mind in the least," he said.

". . . and they'd catch up with us along the road, at the first village you go to for your work. Which one is it?"

"Saint-Irénée."

"I'll tell them. They'll meet up with us and that way you won't have to come back here."

"Thank you," he said.

She'd thought of everything. She suggested they leave in half an hour and have a picnic on the island that afternoon. Along with Slim and the singer, she would prepare the lunch; he wouldn't have to do a thing.

An hour later, disembarking from the ferry they had boarded at Saint-Joseph-de-la-Rive, the Driver and his three passengers arrived at Île aux Coudres. They drove up the hill from the wharf and set out to tour the island.

The Driver went slowly so they could savor the peaceful atmosphere that bathed the island and admire the low stone houses, the old mills, the fields of wildflowers, and the sea birds. Marie was sitting on the stool beside him. Mélodie and Slim, leaning against one another, shared the passenger seat. The singer had dark circles under her eyes from lack of sleep; the acrobat, unshaven and disheveled, had his left arm around her shoulders.

The island was quiet, the tourists few in number. Several times they saw a schooner washed up on the shore, fallen onto its side, of no use any more. The sky was cloudless, the river calm, the air soft and warm.

At the headland just past the Auberge du Capitaine, the Driver found a spot that gave easy access to the shore. He parked the bookmobile, then suggested that the others look for a bay suitable for a picnic while he made a thermos of coffee. At the same time he wanted to check and see if any books had fallen off the shelves during the very steep descent from Les Éboulements to Saint-Joseph-de-la-Rive.

"I'll give you a hand," said Marie. She turned to Slim and Mélodie, who had climbed out of the bus. "You don't mind?" she asked.

"Not at all," said Slim. "See you there."

"Right, see you there," she said.

"See you soon," said Mélodie.

The acrobat and the singer walked away from the shore, each of them holding one handle of the food basket covered with a red-and-white checked tablecloth.

The Driver first made sure that all the books were still on the shelves, then he made coffee and Marie poured it into the thermos. He placed it in a small backpack, along with plastic cups and a package of LU cookies, Marie's favorite, of which he'd bought an assortment before leaving Quebec.

She put her hand on his shoulder.

"Thank you for the cookies. It was sweet of you to remember."

"Don't mention it," he said, bringing his shoulder up slightly and his head down so he could brush his cheek against Marie's hand for a moment.

They got out. As he was closing the back doors he noticed a cat under the van.

"Look, we've got company!" he said.

Marie bent down to look. It was a young black cat with some white on its paws.

"It must be the cat from the inn," she said. "I saw him on the lawn a while ago when we drove past it."

They started to walk along the silent shore. The tide was going out, exposing a sandbar that was dark slate grey, nearly black. Slim and Mélodie were nowhere in sight; they were probably a little farther away, looking for a soft sand cove. The Driver glanced behind him.

"The little cat's following us," he said.

They stopped and the cat did too. He had a white spot on his muzzle that looked like a big drop of milk. He seemed to be very busy playing in the puddles, but when they moved on he again started to follow them.

A rocky barrier stood in front of them. They crossed it and then for the fun of it hid behind a big stump. A few moments later the little black cat ran up to them, looking absolutely lost. Spying them by the stump he took a detour and veered off towards the river.

Just as they were getting back on their path they saw the acrobat and the singer lying in the sand at the end of a cove. They were on their sides, facing on another; their eyes were closed and they seemed to be asleep. They'd taken off their shoes and their T-shirts. Both were very white, except for their tanned faces, necks and fore-arms. They had stowed the picnic basket in the shadow of the rock closest to them.

Marie seemed moved by the sight; her breathing was rapid. On tiptoe, the Driver went over and set his backpack down near the picnic basket, then came back, took her by the arm and led her to the other side of the cove. They sat on the sandy shore with their backs against a rock. Immediately the black cat, breathless from running to the river, climbed onto a round rock a few meters from them. He began to lick his muddy paws.

"They both look so fragile . . ." said Marie.

"Yes, they do," he said.

Still in the grip of her emotion, she frowned and nervously drew something in the sand. He put his shoulder against hers, inviting her to lean on him if she felt the need. Gradually she calmed down.

All at once the little cat jumped off his rock and started running again towards the water's edge.

"There are birds over there," she said.

"Where?" he asked.

"There, between the pointed rock and the round one."

She pointed to a specific spot at the edge of the water, but though he opened his eyes very wide, using his hands as a visor to protect them from the sun, he could see nothing.

"I don't see them," he said.

"They're at the edge of the water. They have delicate feet and take quick little steps. They're killdeer."

"I can't see a thing," he said unhappily. "How do you do it?"

"Oh, I'm used to it."

"How come?"

"I paint birds."

She spoke naturally as if it was a profession that you came across every day, but the Driver was flabbergasted.

"Do you really paint birds?" he asked.

"Of course. It's my job."

"Like Audubon?"

"If you want. Did you know that he came here to the North Shore?"

He shook his head. She told him that Audubon had explored the shore from Natashquan to Badore in the summer of 1833, on board the schooner *Ripley*, and that he'd brought back twenty or so drawings of birds from that expedition.

"I had no idea," said the Driver. "I've seen reproductions of his paintings . . . I've always wondered how he could be so precise."

"He had a method . . . that you won't be happy to hear about," said Marie.

"What was that?"

"I'm sorry to tell you, but to study birds up close he would shoot them. And then use wires to keep them in position."

"Oh no!"

"That was the technique they used in the nineteenth century. Nowadays we use binoculars. It takes a little more patience . . ."

Interrupted by shouting, she turned her head. Slim and Mélodie, sitting in the middle of a big puddle twenty meters from them on the sandbar, were splashing each other, whooping and laughing.

"They're so good together," she murmured.

Because of the sun her eyes were half-closed and it was impossible for the Driver to tell what feelings were troubling her soul. But her face was relaxed and she seemed very calm.

"They'll be famished," she said, getting to her feet. "Come, let's take out the food and set up our picnic."

"All right," he said. "But some day, when you're in the mood, will you tell me how you go about your work? How you identify the birds, how you approach them and all that?"

"I'll be glad to," she said.

"Thank you."

He was looking at her with such obvious admiration that she couldn't help smiling. Since he was standing there, unmoving, she took his hand and led him to the rock where they'd stowed their provisions. He didn't take his eyes off her while she picked up the clothes that the other two had left on the sand where they'd slept. Eventually he got a grip on himself. He helped her spread the red-and-white checked tablecloth and lay out the sandwiches, coffee, cookies, and utensils.

Slim and Mélodie came running, naked and soaking wet, and the little black cat was not far behind.

A VERY EASY DEATH

THE BOOKMOBILE was parked on the wharf at Saint-Iréné. For the first time since the beginning of the journey, the Driver was alone. The band members, who had met them at the location set by Marie, had then left with her for La Malbaie where they were thinking of doing a show.

It was late afternoon. All day the Driver's mood had been as changeable as the river, which went from grey to green depending on the intensity of the light. It hadn't kept him from greeting cordially all the readers who turned up – elderly people, schoolchildren, tourists. The head of his network, however, hadn't arrived yet.

The head of the Saint-Irénée network was a woman of forty or so, named Madeleine, a former librarian. The network – one of the most extensive in the region – had no fewer than twenty-seven members spread across an area demarcated by the villages of Saint-Joseph-de-la-Rive, Point-au-Pic, and Saint-Aimé-des-Lacs.

To pass the time he switched on the radio, choosing FM with the thought of listening to some music, but the first thing he heard was a literary program about Céline. A professor of literature with a deep, warm voice was commenting on passages from *Journey to the End of Night*. After that, he talked about how one night after eating, Céline had felt tired. "I'm going to lie down for a while," he'd said. Later, the writer had added: "I must remember to mail my letters." And then he passed away. It had been a very easy death.

The program ended and was followed by classical music, then some songs. The Driver turned up the volume and went outside to have a closer look at the river and to smell the salt water. The wharf was being repaired, but as it was after six, the workers had finished for the day and only two fishermen were there at the end of the jetty, casting their lines far out into the river. The Driver chatted with them for a while. Then, spotting Madeleine's pink Volvo, he went back to the bookmobile.

She got out of the car with a pile of books in her arms and smiled at the Driver, who was coming towards her.

"I saw the bookmobile on my way home from shopping," she said.

"Bonjour!" he said. "Just a minute, I'll turn down the radio."

"No, wait . . ."

It was a song she knew, one of Alain Souchon's, all subtlety and half-tones. She closed her eyes and began to sing softly:

When I'm knocked out of the ring
And there's no one to hear when I sing
When I'm down on the floor
And someone who's tougher
And younger's lookin' down on me
Will you still love me
Like you did before?

When the song was over, the Driver hurried to take the books from Madeleine. He got into the bookmobile with her, placed the books on the folding table and turned off the radio. Then he put his hands on the woman's hips and, standing on tiptoe, kissed her gently on the cheeks. She was very tall, with a radiant face, big blue eyes and blonde hair pulled into a bun.

"I'm terribly late," she said. "Sorry."

"That's quite all right," he said.

"Thanks."

"How did you like the books?"

"I liked them a lot. We all did," she said, smiling.

She waved her arms as she spoke and the library seemed to have shrunk.

"Is everyone well?" he asked, concerned.

"No," she said, and her smile froze. "Georges isn't well."

"Is it serious?"

"He's in the hospital."

Georges was the oldest member of the network. Though the Driver had never met him, he'd heard so much about him that he thought of the man as a friend. He had been wounded in the Second World War and he had asthma. It was harder and harder for him to breath and, in addition, the cortisone he had to take had affected his digestive system.

While not essential, George's position in the network was important: five other readers came after him.

"Don't lose faith," she said. "He's been through worse, old Georges. He'll certainly come out of it. For the time being his daughter is looking after the books. Her name is Louise."

"Of course," he said.

He admired Madeleine. Not only was she one of those women who finds a solution for everything, but also her reading experience was much broader than his. She'd read a great many little-known authors, who weren't discussed in the literary magazines and who came from places as varied as South Africa, Iceland, Australia, and Eastern Europe.

Chingiz Aitmatov, for instance. She had long been familiar with the work of the writer from Kyrgyzstan, a country that was once part of the USSR and was situated northwest of China, on the old Silk Road. She'd had him read *Jamilia*, *The White Ship*, and *Blue Mouse*,

Bring Me Water and he had fallen in love with everything by that writer, whose existence he'd been unaware of until then.

"Thanks for telling me about old Georges," he said.

She bowed her head and her smile reappeared.

"I owed you that," she said. "Wasn't it you who taught me that all readers are important, even the ones at the end of the line?"

"I don't remember," he said, smiling in turn.

She always talked about the "line" or the "chain." He preferred the word "network" though, but never used it in front of her or anyone else. It was a word that he kept for himself, a word that evoked the Resistance and the Occupation, which he only knew about from movies and from Vercors's book *The Silence of the Sea*.

"Can I offer you something to drink?" he asked. "A glass of wine perhaps? Rosé . . ."

"Oh, yes!" she said. "Thank you."

Sliding the shelf unit away from the kitchen nook, he served the rosé; then, carrying his glass, he went to sit in the back doorway. Madeleine had started to pick some new books and it was a pleasure to see how comfortable she was in the library. She'd pick up the books, leaf through them, stroke them, talk to them, and breathe in their odor. Bathed in the soft light spread by the sun as it set behind the village, she turned around, searching through all the shelves, pausing briefly to sip her wine.

While she was making her selection, he went to the cab and

opened his black notebook to the page for the Saint-Irénée network. To makes things easier for the person who would be replacing him, he wrote the name Louise, in parentheses, under that of Georges, then at the bottom of the page he noted everything Madeleine had told him about the new reader. After that he replaced the notebook in the glove compartment.

As he was going back to the library, he noticed that Madeleine had picked Jack's latest novel. She also took a collection of Raymond Carver's short stories, *Will You Please Be Quiet, Please*; a John Fante, *Ask the Dust*; a Louis Gauthier, *Voyage en Irlande avec un parapluie*; a Philippe Dijan, *Échine*; a Pierre Morency, *L'Oeil américain*; a Francine Noël, *Maryse*; several novels by beginning writers and two books for children published by La Courte Échelle.

"I have to stop," she said.

"As you wish," he said. "There's no limit."

"Someone asked me for some recipes. May I take the Chinese cookbook?"

"Of course you can," he said, smiling.

"And I'd also like a manuscript. It's been ages since I've read one."

"Of course."

He drained his glass and got up to open the chest full of manuscripts that had been turned down, which was in the cab behind the passenger seat. He was careful not to make a mistake: the other chest, the one on the driver's side, contained mainly the tools for the truck; it also held some flexible, fire-resistant tubing long enough to reach from the tail pipe to the window in the driver's door.

A GOOD CUP OF COFFEE
AT LA MALBAIE

Two days later, the Driver met up with Marie and the band at La Malbaie. He had no trouble finding them – once again, they'd set up camp behind the church.

That evening, they put on a show.

To begin, Mélodie sang a naïve and simple song called "Les Amants de la Saint-Jean," accompanied by just an accordion. The spectators applauded but with restraint, as if they didn't want to disturb her. But from the gleam in their eyes and the smiles that lit up their faces it was easy to see that they were moved.

The musicians had positioned themselves in front of an oak tree with no low branches so that people watching the show could look out at the River behind the troupe. Among the spectators was Madeleine, who'd come from Saint-Irénée with a group of children. Happy to see her again, the Driver seated himself beside her, on a sleeping bag she'd spread out on the grass. As usual, Marie was in the front row, from where she discreetly saw to it that the show ran smoothly. As the air off the river was cool, he'd lent her a long woolen scarf that she had wrapped twice around her neck.

After Mélodie came the jugglers' act, accompanied by the band playing softly. It was a show they'd done before, but that evening the moves were so precise, so smooth, they seemed effortless; in fact they appeared to be executing them in slow motion. And when all four jugglers sent the bowling pins back and forth, crisscrossing, there was magic in the way the objects spun in the air with a faint hissing sound and brushed against each other but never touched.

The next to step up were the man and woman who did tricks with the black dog. The man took a harmonica from his pocket and began to play a tune that had been popular years before, "How Much Is That Doggie in the Window?" The woman sang the verses in a clear voice and at the chorus, the dog punctuated every sentence by barking twice, which made the children laugh a lot, and then the parents. After that, the show took on a friendly and intimate air. The three of them formed a pyramid, the woman climbing on to the man's back on her hands and knees, and the dog onto the woman's. At the end, the man skipped rope while the band played a rousing tune and the dog began on his own to dance along with him. What the three of them did was funny and light and filled with good-natured humor. Even the black dog, with his golden eyes that shone now and then under a tousled tuft of hair, didn't appear to take himself seriously:

he wasn't a circus animal but an intelligent, energetic, and somewhat undisciplined mutt.

Then came the climax of the show. Slim had prepared his material: he'd spread all his juggler's articles on the ground, soaked his torches in gasoline, checked the rigidity of the cable strung between the oak tree and a metal post. Now he was sitting motionless on the ground with his eyes closed, legs folded, palms turned up. He was concentrating or meditating. Either that or simply watching the sun go down and waiting for nightfall.

When he climbed up on the cable and began to walk, arms stretched out on either side, head erect and eyes focused on the river – so broad here that the other shore was barely visible – all at once he seemed vulnerable and frail. At the end, though, when he juggled with knives and flaming torches while maintaining his balance, he was like a magician writing letters of fire on the black sky.

Though the show had been over for a while people were in no hurry to leave. Some were examining the musical instruments, others were talking with the singer or playing with the dog, while still others were helping Slim and the jugglers carry their equipment to the school bus. Madeleine was among the last to leave, taking along in her Volvo the children from Saint-Irénée who'd come with her. Before climbing into her car she turned around and waved a long goodbye to the Driver; from the way the children were pressing around her you could tell that they liked her a lot.

When everyone had gone and the equipment had been put away, Marie came over to the Driver. "The take was good," she said. "We'd like you to be our guest at the little café on the road not far from here."

"I was very glad to see you again," he said, "and the show was magical – but I'm not really in the mood to be with a group tonight. There are some dark thoughts inside my head. Do you understand?"

"Of course."

"Will we see each other tomorrow?"

"We certainly will."

"I'll have a bite to eat in the van, then I'll take a walk along the river."

She stroked his forehead gently, wished him *bon appétit* and a pleasant walk, then she joined the others who were making their way along the road.

He cooked up some spaghetti, having first opened the window in the roof so the steam wouldn't damage the books. He had cookies and applesauce for dessert, then set out along the shore. After walking for no more than five minutes, he was shrouded in a patch of fog. He continued to walk for a while, following the wrack line from the last tide, but soon the damp air was seeping into him and he went back onto the road.

The sight of a phone booth under a streetlamp suddenly gave him an urge to talk to Jack. He swung open the door, inserted a coin and punched in his friend's number.

"Hello?" said a voice.

It was Rachel.

"Bonsoir," he said. "It's the Driver."

"Bonsoir. Where are you?"

"La Malbaie. Is Jack there?"

"No, he's on the North Shore. He left a note to say he was going to Baie-Comeau. He's doing research for a novel."

"Did he say when he'd be there?"

"No. You know what he's like . . . I found his note when I came back from a trip."

"I understand," he said.

"Do you want to leave a message?"

"No, that's all right."

"Okay. How's the summer tour going?"

"Very well. How are things with the Indians?"

"Not too bad," she said.

"Well . . . take care of yourself!"

"You too!"

He hung up, shivering from the dampness, and resumed his walk along the road. A few minutes later he saw the blinking blue lights of the café Marie had mentioned.

As he pushed open the door he was assailed by the overly loud music from the jukebox, but as it was an old Elvis song, "Good Luck Charm," he went in anyway. All the booths were occupied by people from the troupe. He made a vague gesture with his hand that could be interpreted as a greeting to everyone, including Marie, who was sitting across from Slim, and sat on the first stool at the counter.

The music stopped. Slim stood up and invited the Driver to take his place.

"I don't want to disturb you," said the Driver in a low voice.

"You won't," said Slim, shaking his hand. "We've finished."

"Thanks."

"We were talking about the future," said Marie, who was folding a road map of Quebec.

Slim turned and went to sit in another booth where Mélodie and the man and woman with the black dog were already seated.

"So . . . how was your walk?" asked Marie.

"It was chilly because of the fog," he said, rubbing his hands together.

She put her hands around his to warm them, then took them away when the waitress came to take their orders. Both asked for hot chocolate. They talked about this and that until the waitress came back with the two steaming cups. The chocolate was very good and the Driver, who was usually not very talkative, began to recount his travels in France some time ago. He had bought an old van and lived in it at three different spots: Paris, Tournon-sur-Rhône, and Le Verdon, at the mouth of the Gironde.

"Did you like Paris?" she asked.

"A lot. I felt at home there because I'd read Hemingway's book, *A Moveable Feast*. Have you read it?"

"Of course," she said.

He shook his head, laughing quietly.

"Can I tell you something?" he asked.

"Sure."

"You talk like me. You say, 'Of course' and 'Sure.' And you've read the same books I have . . . How come we're so much alike, you and I?"

"I have no idea," she said, smiling. He saw a little glimmer deep in her grey-blue eyes.

"I've forgotten what I was talking about," he said.

"You were talking about Hemingway and Paris."

"Ah, yes . . . When I got to Paris I went to the places where Hemingway had lived. I took his book and followed the same route: up Cardinal-Lemoine to La Contrescarpe, across the Place du Panthéon, I walked for a while along boulevard Saint-Michel, then I turned onto the little rue de l'Odéon to follow him into Shakespeare and Company. And . . . do you know what?"

"What?" asked Marie.

"All those places, especially the Place de la Contrescarpe, were even more wonderful than they'd been in my dreams. I mean, reading *A Moveable Feast* had filled my head with beautiful images, but in the end reality was much better than anything I'd imagined. The only exception was Shakespeare and Company . . ."

"It was less beautiful?"

"No, it had moved. It was no longer on rue de l'Odéon. I looked for it for a long time and finally found it on the quays, on rue de la Bûcherie across from Notre-Dame. I took a photo. Night was falling and . . ."

"Is that the photo in the bookmobile, above the sink?"

"Yes."

"I like it a lot," she said. "The night is blue and because the bookstore is lit from inside, it's as if that golden light comes from the books . . . as if the books themselves are making the light burst out."

"That's exactly what I wanted to say and I'd have used the same words. I swear."

"I believe you," she said, putting her hand over her heart.

They took a long sip of hot chocolate before it cooled down, then sat in silence for a long moment, looking at each other in awe. Finally, he asked:

"Know what I'm thinking about?"

"No," she said.

"I'm thinking about another chapter in Hemingway's book, the one entitled 'A Good Cup of Coffee on the Place Saint-Michel.'

The author is in a café, he's writing a story and drinking St. James rum to warm up. A young girl is sitting in a corner. He thinks she's beautiful, he goes on writing his story and he feels good . . . Do you remember?"

"Of course."

"Now it's as if we're both inside Hemingway's book," he said.

She nodded in agreement and they both finished their hot chocolate, even the last mouthful, which is always slightly bitter.

PORT-AU-PERSIL

H E WAS DRIVING towards Port-au-Persil. Marie was with him, though she wasn't supposed to have come so far: it had been agreed that the bookmobile would stop where the road branched off into the village and that she'd go back to the school bus, because her friends in the band wanted to go to Tadoussac and join a whale-watching excursion.

Because of the morning fog that refused to lift, they couldn't see the River, but they could spot purple patches of fireweed along the road and in the fields and ditches. By consulting *La Flore Laurenti-enne*, which Marie had just discovered, they learned that the precise name for the color of these flowers was magenta.

Marie was holding the book by Frère Marie-Victorin on her lap and was turning the pages, looking at the illustrations and reading phrases at random.

"It's beautiful and well-written," she said. "Did he write other books?"

"Yes," he said. "I read something about the North Shore by him. It's in a book by a writer named . . . Hold on, the title is . . ."

But though he searched his memory, he could recall neither the title nor the author's name. That was happening more and more often and it irritated him.

"The book's on the shelf," he said.

"Let's trade places and I'll go and get it."

She hurried to put down *La Flore Laurentienne* and take over the wheel, because he'd already left his place to go into the library. Without losing her composure she seated herself and stepped on the gas, turning the wheel to correct a swerve. Luckily, the road was nearly straight. Unaware of the danger, he came back proudly with the book; It was La Côte-Nord dans la Littérature, by Mgr René Bélanger.

"It's wonderful," he said, "listen to this." Sitting down, he started to read, very slowly:

> *The powerful musculature of the planet, flayed and stripped*
> *bare by the patient action of countless centuries; a rose granite*
> *forehead marked only by an eyebr ow of greyish lichen, a stub-*
> *born brow against which the cold blue sea tirelessly conveys*
> *legions of white rams from offshore; a wonderfully luminous*
> *sky where prevails the cold Atlantic breezes laden with the*
> *harsh scents of the Arctic tundra; the shrill and exhilarating*

*symphony of myriads of birds pecking hungrily at the inex-
haustible feeding station of the sea, then flying back obliquely
to their rocky ledge; and finally, behind the low horizon, a
flat, unending desert that recedes to the vacant North: these,
it seems, are the key features in the image of the North Shore
as it appears to the traveler who, from a small fishing boat,
follows that interminable shore at close quarters for days at
a time.*

"That's very beautiful," Marie agreed. "It makes you want to go there."

"You'll be there soon: the North Shore more or less begins at Tadoussac."

He set the book on the dashboard with *La Flore Laurentienne* and then, for no apparent reason, he was locked away inside himself, suddenly silent and melancholy. Marie was aware of it.

"You've stopped reading?"

"I'm not in the mood."

"Do you want to drive?"

"No."

"Do you want me to tell you something?"

"Yes."

"I'll tell you how the band got started, okay?"

"Okay."

Marie was a very good driver. Highway 138 was tortuous and uneven in places, but she used the gearshift skillfully on the curves and on the hills, and she was quite capable of telling her story while she drove and even of glancing at the river when the road hugged the indentations along the shore.

It had started in the area around Tournon where she lived, when a dozen old friends (a cabinetmaker, a luthier, a photographer, a musician, a plumber, an architect, a mechanic) began to lament that money had taken priority in their lives. The people around them thought about nothing but money and they themselves had carelessly fallen into the same way of thinking.

In reaction, they had put together the band. Those who played an instrument taught the rudiments to the others. They got together every weekend to play music. One evening they'd met Slim, who later joined them and shared with them his interest in juggling. Mélodie, the last arrival, had brought a new energy to the group.

"And you?" he asked. "You've forgotten to talk about yourself . . ."

"Me? I didn't do anything special. I didn't even play an instrument, except for castanets and tambourine . . ."

"The what?"

"The tambourine. It's like a wooden hoop with little bells all around it."

"Oh, right. But how did you become the group's manager?"

Marie slowed down to drive through a village, lost in the fog, called Saint-Fidèle.

I'm not really the manager. But there's a big living room in my house, so they got in the habit of coming there to play. And little by little I took over the practical details. Someone had to, especially when they started touring."

"What about the cats, weren't they afraid when you were playing music?"

"Yes," she said, "they'd climb the ladder and hide at the back of the shed, but gradually they got used to it."

"Sorry to interrupt," he said. "You were talking about tours . . . "

"Yes. At first they'd play in nearby villages, then they gained more confidence and one day we bought an old bus, quite similar to the school bus but smaller, and painted green. We fixed it up and decorated it and then we travelled and played in various countries: Holland, Belgium, Switzerland, Italy, Spain . . ."

"You mean the musicians quit their jobs?"

"Of course."

"You too?"

"It's different for me. When we travel I always bring a sketchbook and pencils, so I can make sketches. This time I even brought my binoculars and a tripod. I'll bring them out soon . . . I mustn't be too rusty when I go back to France at the beginning of September, because I have a job waiting."

"A job?" he repeated in a voice that – he couldn't help it – was rather unsteady.

"Nothing's been signed, it's a trial contract with a magazine."

"Are you . . . are you famous?" he asked, searching for his words.

"No," she replied, laughing. "I'm known to a few people who are very fond of birds."

"And that's enough for you?"

"Yes. What about you?"

"What?" he asked.

"Are you well-known?"

"No. Just to some people who are very fond of books."

"And that suits you?"

He shrugged, trying to think. A road sign announced that they would soon be at Port-au-Persil.

"What would suit me," he said, "would be . . . if time could stop."

She held out her hand to him but they'd already reached the road that led to the village. Immediately she turned right, stopped the van a little further along, half on the shoulder, and switched on the warning lights because of the fog.

"I hope the fog lifts," she said, "or we won't be able to see the whales. But I'm not even sure I want to see them— I mean, maybe it's better to leave them in peace."

"Do you think so?"

"What I think is, I'd rather stay with you."

"You can stay if you want."

"But you see, I can't always leave the others. You understand that, don't you?"

"Of course . . . Look, the leaves are stirring, there's a little wind now."

The sound of an engine on the road made them turn their heads.

It was not the bus but a huge truck full of gravel. They listened to the deafening noise, which went on for a while before it faded away, then the Driver wondered out loud if he had time to make coffee. He hesitated and just as he was getting up to put the water on, the yellow bus pulled up with all its lights flashing and stopped on the main road just past the turnoff.

Marie hastened to get out.

"Goodbye!" she said.

"Bye! Good luck with the readers!"

Anxiously, he watched her go. She waved to him as she boarded the bus, which drove off at once. Before starting up again, the Driver got out and looked under the van. No cats. He got in, started the van and drove slowly into Port-au-Persil. Under the fog that was now unravelling in the late morning, the inhabitants were quietly engaged in their daily tasks; a man who was fixing his roof waved when he saw the bookmobile drive by. After a stop to buy groceries, he turned into the narrow winding road that would take him to the wharf.

It was only a bit of a dock that projected modestly into the middle of a small bay, but the place was so restful that the Driver was always eager to get back there. On his arrival he saw a painter who had set up his easel on the left, so he parked on the other side, as far from the artist as possible. He opened the two back doors to wait for the head of the network or any other reader.

When the fog was dispersing, he spied to the right of the wharf a sailboat and a few small craft bobbing on the green water, and to the left, a landscape of pink rocks with a white frame house and a little chapel in the background: it was the landscape reproduced on the artist's canvas.

The painter was an old man with a weather-beaten complexion. Not wanting to disturb his concentration, the Driver dared not get out, but he could see through the window that the artist was working in watercolor and that his hand was trembling. He decided to act as if Marie were there and launched into a conversation with her.

"Look," he said. "A colleague of yours . . . Do you like what he's doing?"

"It's good. Especially the rocks. Rocks are very difficult."

"Are they?"

"Because the shapes are so varied and imprecise."

"True. So the white house and the little chapel are easier?"

"Of course. See how clearly the roofs stand out against the blue of the sky."

It really did feel as if Marie were in the van with him. They were talking *sotto voce* so as not to disturb the painter.

"I hope my network head won't get here too soon. His old moped makes a lot of noise."

"What does he do?"

"He's a carpenter."

"And the network operates well?"

"Yes, it's very stable. There aren't a lot of members, just eleven, but they're all faithful readers."

The artist had finished his painting. He cleaned his brushes, folded his easel and stowed everything in a big khaki-colored bag. The Driver got out of the van to say hello to him. The painting was leaning against a wooden beam that served as a guardrail.

"Congratulations!" said the Driver. "That's very fine."

"Oh," said the painter, "it's nothing much!"

"But it's well done, with the fog and everything."

"Thank you."

The old man slung the bag over his shoulder.

"I'll be back in a while," he said. "I've got something for you."

With that, he slowly walked away, holding his painting by one corner.

The Driver took his black notebook from the glove compartment and sat on the wharf to study the Port-au-Persil network in detail. The fog had dissipated and the warmth of the sun felt good. He studied his notes for a while, then began to feel hungry. His watch showed half-past twelve. As there weren't any readers he decided to fix himself a ham sandwich with the raisin bread he'd just bought. He drank some vegetable juice first and he was grilling the bread on the camping toaster when he heard footsteps on the wharf. It was a boy and a girl, wearing brightly colored jogging clothes and holding hands, who'd come on foot.

He didn't know them and their appearance didn't match that of any member of the network described in the black notebook. They were probably in the category that he mentally called solitary readers.

They approached him.

"Can we have some books?" asked the girl.

"Sure," he said. "Just a second."

They were sixteen or seventeen, both with long blond hair haloed with lights. Both were incredibly beautiful. The Driver took the two slices of bread and even though they were only toasted on one side, he buttered them and placed a slice of ham between them: the ham hung out of the sandwich on all sides but he didn't have time to fix it. He took a can of Canada Dry from the fridge, stacked his dirty dishes in the sink and moved the shelving unit so it would hide the kitchen nook.

"There you go," he said, "I'll let you choose." He got out of the van with his still-warm sandwich and his ginger ale. So as not to disturb them he went and sat at the end of the wharf.

He ate heartily, watching the boats go by and tossing bits of bread at the gulls soaring overhead. He'd just finished his lunch when the young couple came to show him what they'd chosen. Two very serious books, *Hour of Our Delight*, by Hubert Reeves, and *Option Québec*, by René Lévesque. They wanted to know how to return them after they'd read them. The Driver explained that they could send them to the Ministry in Quebec City. He offered them something to drink, but they were in a hurry and took off with their books, still holding hands. Soon they were only a spot of bright color that disappeared, then reappeared, along the winding road to the wharf.

During the afternoon, the Driver had visits from a handful of other solitary readers; some came from the village, others were tourists. Though he wasn't quite so fond of the latter he did his best to treat everyone with equal courtesy. The head of the network, who didn't have much work in the carpentry shop, turned up on his putt-putting moped around three o'clock. He praised the books he'd brought back. Through some roundabout questions, the Driver learned that the little network was doing well. He let the carpenter pick some new titles, then joined him in a beer. He set great store by doing his work as well as he usually did and not letting his own concerns show.

Late that afternoon, just as time was beginning to slow down, he was sitting by himself in the back of the van when he saw the old man who had painted the watercolor. His arms were full of books.

"Hello again," said the Driver.

"These are for you," said the painter.

He came up and set the pile of books on the floor of the van. At first glance the Driver saw several titles that he recognized.

"Are you lending them to me?" he asked.

"No, giving them. I don't need them any more."

"But . . . are you sure?"

"Yes. I'm sick . . . And I don't have any children."

The Driver looked at the books one by one. He could hardly believe his eyes: with a few exceptions, these were books that had delighted and nourished his own youth: *Robinson Crusoe*; *The Little Prince*; *Menaud, maître-draveur*; *LÉtranger dans la patrouille*; a volume of the *Encylopédie de la jeunesse*; *The Last of the Mohicans*; *Treasure Island* and some others, including an old editions of *La Flore Laurentienne*.

"And now I have to be going," said the painter.

The Driver spent a long time watching the man go away; he seemed tired and his back was bent. He looked so old . . . And yet, judging by the books he'd left, the man must have been around his own age. Under the shock of his emotions, he resumed his conversation with Marie.

"Did you see that?" he asked. "They're the same books I read when I was little! Do I look as old as that man?"

"Hardly," she said.

"And there was even a *Flore Laurentienne*."

"You're in luck."

"Do you think so? . . . I'm giving it to you then. It's yours."

"Thank you very much," she said. "I can't imagine a more precious gift. It's as if you were giving me all the flowers of Quebec."

He smiled a little sadly, shelved the books and went back to sit by himself at the end of the wharf.

LIGHT FROM BOOKS

WHEN HE ARRIVED at the mouth of the Saguenay he could see in the distance that the ferry was still at the dock; he sped up and had just enough time to drive the bookmobile on board. As he did during every tour, he saluted the round-backed mountains at the foot of which emerged the swift, dark water of the river, and he listened to the boat's motor whose muffled, rhythmic sound always reminded him of the beating of a human heart. All at once, halfway through the crossing, as he was looking in the direction of Tadoussac, he spotted the yellow bus near the wharf and his own heart began to beat faster.

On the opposite shore, after hesitating briefly and trying to see if the musicians were there, he parked the van next to the bus. Marie was sitting at a window, apparently absorbed in some task. She looked up and gave him a smile that was an invitation to come in. He took a deep breath: she was alone.

"Shall I shut the door to keep the mosquitoes out?" he asked, stepping inside.

She nodded. Now in early August there weren't many mosquitoes but closing the compressed-air door of the old bus gave great satisfaction to the Driver as well as to the members of the band. And so he settled into the driver's seat and, firmly grasping the metal handle that activated the folding door, he pulled it towards him. The door closed with its characteristic *whsshh*.

"Have a seat," said Marie.

She was hunched over a pad of writing paper, wearing glasses with very fine blue rims that accentuated her grave and gentle appearance. He sat down across from her.

"Am I disturbing you?" he asked.

"Not at all, I've finished."

She wrote another few words and signed her name.

"I'm an expert at reading upside down," he said, and read aloud: "I send you all my love and a big hug."

She separated the pages, folded them, and slipped them into an envelope, then she addressed it.

"It's to my parents," she said, sealing the envelope.

"Ah . . . you still have your parents?"

"Yes."

She looked at him closely and he didn't have to tell her that his own were no longer alive. She offered him coffee; he said yes and she got up to open the curtain to the kitchen. The people in the band had put in a very simple system of curtains that slide along rails to divide the space into several sections: kitchen, bedroom, parlor.

When the coffee was ready she brought the cups into the parlor and set them on the table.

"Thank you," he said. "How were the whales? Did you see any?"

"Yes," she said. "They're very impressive. The others went back today to see them again. They were hoping to see a blue whale."

"And you didn't go?"

"I had letters to write. And then I . . . I didn't want you to find the bus empty when you got here."

"That's so nice of you," he said. He took a long sip of coffee. "Your coffee's better than mine!"

Reaching out to touch his arm, the way she often did, she asked: "Will you be staying in Tadoussac to work?"

"No," he said. "I'm going to Les Escoumins."

"That's not very far, is it?"

"Quite close, but it's a difficult drive so I'll be leaving fairly soon . . . What about you?"

"We're staying for a while, then we're going to do a show in Baie-Comeau."

"You are? I'll be there too! I stop there during every tour to stock up on books: it's about halfway . . . And Jack may be there too."

"So we may see each other . . . Would you like a bite to eat before you go?"

"I don't know. Will your friends be back soon?"

"Not right away."

"Then I'll have a cookie or two."

She went to look for the bag of LU cookies in the kitchen.

"Thank you," he said. "There's something I want to tell you but I can't find the words."

"Take all the time you need," she said.

He munched some cookies, looking at the river and at the excursion boats going in one direction or another.

"All right," he said. "Do you remember what we talked about that night on the Île d'Orléans, when we were at the top of the observation tower?"

"Yes . . ."

"Well, I haven't changed my mind; I'm still not interested in old age. On the other hand, I've never had such a wonderful tour and I know that it's because of you. I always look forward to seeing you. I think about you and when you aren't there I miss you; sometimes I even talk to you."

"Same here," she said.

"I wonder how I've been able to get along without you till now . . . That's what I wanted to tell you."

They looked at one another in silence for a moment, each one happy because of what they saw in the other's eyes. Then he said:

"Do you know what your bus makes me think of when we're inside?"

"No," she said.

"With the row of windows, it reminds me of the sun porch that we had when I was a child. That's where I discovered books. It was a very special place."

He described the long sun porch with the bookshelves at either end, the wicker chairs, the small desk, and the row of windows with a shelf underneath where you could rest your feet. The porch was closed in winter and opened again in the spring, as soon as the sun was warm enough. He'd spent part of his childhood reading in that room flooded with light, sitting in a deep armchair with his feet resting on the window ledge. And over time, because the sun had brightened him and warmed him while he was reading, his mind had associated light with books.

"That's why I wasn't surprised later on when I saw Shakespeare and Company in Paris one autumn evening, with the golden light that came from the books and spread into the blue night. It confirmed what I'd known since I was a child. Do you understand?"

"Yes," she said.

"I shouldn't have asked, you always understand . . . Is there any other person in this world as nice as you?"

Her only reply was a smile. They sat there in silence for a while, looking out at the river now and then to see if the musicians were coming back from their excursion. Abruptly he checked the time and stood up.

"I have to go."

"Have a safe journey," she said. "Be careful and don't drive too fast."

"I'll look all over Baie-Comeau for you," he said.

After opening the compressed-air door, he stepped briskly down from the bus. A big yellow tomcat raced away when he started up the engine of the van.

As it left the shore of the river, Highway 1138 climbed into the mountains, hurtled down hills, travelled around Lac Long, Lac Croche, and Lac á Gobert, then climbed up to a sandy plateau and down into a valley of cultivated land; after that, it went back to the St. Lawrence and crossed two rivers before it finally came to Les Escoumins.

The Driver drove the bookmobile to the entrance of the wharf. It was a popular spot because of the ferry that went to Trois-Pistoles on the south shore. Many of the readers there were tourists and travelers. With such people he knew that a certain number of books would never make it back to Quebec City, but it didn't matter: books were constantly moving around and travelling, and it was the best thing that could happen to them. Besides, in compensation there were always some surprising readers who would touch him by offering their own books as gifts . . .

The head of the network didn't arrive until the next day. He was a boat pilot just coming back from work; he piloted heavy tonnage ships that plied the channel in the St. Lawrence between Les Escoumins and Quebec City. His visit was brief but cordial. The Driver got a piece of information that reassured him about the health of the network: whenever the pilot's work took him away, which often happened, his wife looked after the books in his place.

After the man had left, the Driver got back on the road. It ran closer to the river here and passed through half a dozen villages huddled together. He stopped at Les-Îlets-Jérémie. In that hamlet, the network of readers was headed by the postmistress. She arrived at the end of the afternoon, as he'd expected, but after her there were no other readers. He forced himself to stay for another day, but no one showed up. Early the next morning he got on the road to Baie-Comeau, after he had filled up with gas.

THE IMMORTAL MASTERPIECE
BY JAMES FENIMORE COOPER

A T BAIE-COMEAU he went directly to the library, looking to the left and right along the road, trying to spot the yellow bus or his friend Jack's Volkswagen minibus. He didn't see either one. After he had picked up his three cartons of books, he drove all over town until suddenly he spotted Jack's minibus parked on rue Puyjalon.

The old Volks was easy to recognize from its midnight blue paint job and its elevated roof in which Plexiglas windows had been installed. The body was battered and rusted-out and in several spots you could see sheets of tin held on with pop rivets. The rear window was plastered with stickers declaring that it had travelled across America from the Gaspé Peninsula to San Francisco and Key West, by way of Yellowstone, Yosemite, Death Valley, Las Vegas, and the Grand Canyon.

As the curtains were drawn, the Driver couldn't tell whether Jack was inside. He parked the van and knocked at a window. No answer.

Remembering that his friend often used earplugs when he was writing, he knocked again, harder, but in vain. Nearby were a credit union, a restaurant, a bookstore and a grocery store: he checked all these places, starting with the bookstore, but Jack was nowhere to be seen. He left a note for his friend on his windshield and went to the restaurant to wait.

The waitress brought him a coffee which he sipped while he looked through a newspaper someone had left on the counter. When he finished reading he felt hungry and ordered a grilled cheese sandwich, sugar pie with ice cream, and another coffee. His watch showed two p.m. He went to the restroom and one his way back, he heard a song from the hit parade coming from behind a door closed off by a velvet curtain. Pulling aside half of the curtain he saw a dark room with tables arranged in a semicircle around a small stage under a spotlight.

Just as he was taking a seat at the closest table, the song broke off and was replaced by a Hawaiian guitar that evoked the southern seas. The spotlight turned red and a girl climbed onto the stage. She dropped her cigarette, mashed it with her gold high-heeled shoe, then began to dance and take off her clothes to the languorous rhythm of the music.

The stripper didn't dance very well, she swayed her hips rather awkwardly, but one thing about her was very special: her opulent auburn hair that blazed in the light. When his eyes had got used to

the semi-darkness, the Driver looked around him. A dozen spectators of both sexes were distributed among the tables and most were
paying little attention to the girl; they seemed very busy telling each
other funny stories and drinking beer, and there was even a couple
shooting craps.

Suddenly, while he was watching the girl move to one side of the
stage, he noticed a man sitting all by himself at a table in the half-
light. It was Jack. He was writing in a notebook. He looked up now
and then and smiled at the girl, who smiled back.

As soon as the act was finished, the Driver went over to join his
friend.

"Hi!" he said. "How's it going?"

"Great," said Jack, who didn't seem the least bit surprised to see
him and went on writing in his notebook for a moment. "Have a
seat."

"Are you taking notes?" asked the Driver.

"As you can see."

"So you've started a story?"

"I haven't started writing it, but it's in my head. It's just a little
thing off in a corner somewhere, but it will grow, slowly. I have to
give it time . . . Meanwhile, I'm doing whatever I feel like."

"Rachel told me you'd be in Baie-Comeau."

"Rachel?" said Jack. "How is she?"

He got up, pushing his chair back. Whenever anyone said his wife's name in his presence he'd get worried. He went to the rear of the room to phone, then came back smiling.

"She's fine," he said.

He drained his glass and wiped his forehead: he was perspiring as if he'd just escaped some disaster. The waitress came over. She was the girl with the wonderful head of auburn hair. Jack made the introductions and explained about the Driver's work.

"Actually, the two of you do the same thing," she said.

"We do?" asked the Driver.

"I mean, you both give people books."

Jack and the Driver exchanged a look, first bewildered, then pleased.

"Your hair is so beautiful," said the Driver. "Like a wonderful fire in a fireplace."

"That's a nice thing to say . . . What're you drinking?"

"A beer," said Jack.

"Coffee," said the Driver.

The waitress left them.

"How's the summer round going?" asked Jack.

"Very well," said the Driver. "There's a band that's taking the same route as me. Musicians, jugglers . . . I like them a lot. Especially a woman . . . A woman named Marie."

"Oh yes?"

"There's a strange resemblance between us. We're the same age and she could be my double. We're practically twins. And I'm amazed at what's happening to me: I thought my heart had gone to sleep."

"Life is stronger than we are," said Jack. "And we've got all eternity for sleeping."

"Well, you know, it's not that simple."

Jack jotted something in his notebook.

"Why?" he asked.

The Driver tried to explain what he'd meant but words failed him. He confessed: "I can't say. The only words that come to me are meaningless."

The waitress came back and put the beer and the coffee on the table. The Driver paid while Jack jotted something else in his notebook. The room was too dark for him to read upside down: the only light came from the red glow of the spotlight, which attracted the cigarette smoke as well. He gazed at the swirling smoke for a moment, then took a deep breath and sipped some coffee. After that he said: "Your latest book's doing well. Several readers have borrowed it."

"They have?" asked Jack. "Well, too bad for them!"

"Why?"

"It's not an immortal masterpiece by James Fenimore Cooper!"

The Driver lifted his cup in both hands to hide a smile: that was Jack's favorite remark, one that he made after every novel if the time had come when he felt new images and new sensations stirring inside him and had started to hate the book he'd just written and all the ones he'd written before it.

"Why don't they read John Fante?" asked Jack, getting worked up. "Anyone can see, there's more life in a single one of Fante's books than in all of mine put together. Next to his writing mine's so outdated it could have been taken from King Tut's tomb . . . Why don't they read Richard Ford? . . . And Carver's stories? . . . And good old Hemingway? . . . And Gabrielle Roy? . . . And Boris Vian?"

While he was at it he listed all the authors he liked. It wasn't a very long list. He realized it and said rather bitterly:

"As you can see, I don't like much . . ."

"That's not it," said the Driver, "it's just that your tastes are very precise."

"Basically, I don't like literature."

"Really?"

"The only thing I like is the sentence I've just written in my note-book. And when I re-read it tomorrow morning I probably won't like it anymore."

On that, he burst out laughing and it was so contagious that the Driver joined in. The auburn-haired waitress brought another beer and another coffee that they hadn't asked for and stayed and laughed with them for a moment.

After that, though, Jack gradually withdrew until it was impossible to talk to him. The Driver left then, urging the waitress to keep an eye on him. After picking up the note that he'd left on Jack's windshield, he set out again to wander the town in search of the school bus. Not finding it, he went to the supermarket and then, as he was in the habit of doing at certain stages in the tour, he went to a campground for a shower and some creature comforts.

The campground was on the shore of a lake, along the road leading to the Manicouagan dams. Jittery from all the coffee he'd drunk since morning, the Driver did his laundry, put away his groceries, shelved all the books that had returned to him at the municipal library, cleaned the inside of the van and took his shower. After he'd expended all that energy he felt calmer and a little tired and he went and sat beside the lake. It was Friday and the campground was gradually filling up.

Around seven o'clock that night he went back into town. When he got to rue Puyjalon he noticed that Jack's minibus was still parked outside the restaurant. He drove along at random, taking numerous detours because of roadwork, and ended up near the mall where he'd stocked up on groceries. Suddenly he spotted the school bus in the parking lot just across from the supermarket.

While he was looking for a parking space he noticed that the band was in the middle of the show. They'd set up on a small, half-moon-shaped square that everyone going into the stores by the main entrance had to pass. As usual, Marie was in the front row of spectators and even from a distance, he could see that she was enjoying herself as much as they were. Without leaving the van he watched the show, which was as amusing, simple, and lively as ever. There wasn't a big crowd around the band but there was a constant flow of people who showed up, stayed for a moment and left, tossing a bill into the stovepipe hat; it looked like a good take.

After the show, he overcame his shyness and went to say hello to Marie and the musicians. They were happy. They were growing more and more attached to the North Shore, to its inhabitants and to the river, so wide here that they couldn't see the other shore unless it was exceptionally clear. They'd picked up some local history in a museum and they were still amazed at the exploits of Napoléon-Alexandre Comeau who had given his name to the town. They'd been very impressed by a rescue operation Comeau had carried out on the river during the winter of 1886. Slim, surrounded by Marie and Mélodie and three or four musicians, began to tell this story to the Driver.

One January morning, Comeau was on the river in a canoe, hunting seals with his older brother, when a storm came up. Just as they were returning to land he spotted two men in another canoe, hunting seals with his older brother, when a storm came up. Just as they were returning to land he spotted two men in another canoe, who were about to be trapped by the ice. Without hesitating, he went to their rescue, but all at once both canoes got stuck in a formless mass of water and ice . . .

"What do you call that mixture of ice and water that keeps canoes from moving but isn't solid enough to support you?" asked Slim.

"*Frésil*," said the Driver.

"It just occurred to me — maybe you've heard this story before."

"Me? . . . Umm, I'm not sure."

Because of the enthusiasm of Slim and his friends, the Driver didn't want to admit that he'd read an account of the rescue in Yves Thériault's book *King of the North Shore*. The acrobat went on with the rest of the story.

On the river, the wind was icy and all four men had frozen feet and hands. With a great deal of effort, they'd managed to hoist the two canoes onto a big block of ice and lay them on their sides to provide shelter from the wind. After that Comeau had taken charge. With his rifle he shot some ducks that were flying overhead and used their feathers to line the mitts and boots of the men and give them some protection from the cold. And then, since he knew all the secrets of the winds and tides, he'd quickly realized that their only hope of surviving was to cross the river to the south shore. So the men set off, paddling with all their might in the open water, pushing and dragging the canoes across whatever ice they encountered. Comeau had shown them what direction to take, he'd fed them the meat of the ducks, rubbed their frostbite and urged them on, so that two days and two nights later, exhausted but safe and sound, they alighted on the south shore, near Sainte-Anne-des-Monts.

The musicians gathered around Slim and the Driver blew on their fingers and patted each other's backs as if they'd been the ones to spend two days and two nights on the river in mid-winter. Finally they went their separate ways, each one seeing to his own affairs. The Driver stayed with Slim and the two women and tried to find out when he would see Marie again. He learned that the band's first stop would be nearby, on the shore of the Mistassini River where there was a grotto in which a hermit had spent a number of years following a failed love affair, with two cats as his sole companions, living from hunting and fishing, and from what he grew in a small garden. Then the group intended to go to Sept-Îles and the Indian reservation at Maliotenam.

At best, he wouldn't see Marie again for another four or five days, at Maliotenam. He didn't even have the consolation of telling her he would miss her, because Slim and Mélodie didn't seem to want to leave her alone for one moment.

THE WOMEN OF
RIVIÈRE-PENTECÔTE

A FINE RAIN STARTED to fall as he was putting into Baie-Trinité. His mood was melancholy and he felt like talking to his sister, Julie. He stopped at a phone booth.

"Where are you?" asked Julie.

"At the spot where the river is so wide that people call it 'the sea.'"

"At Pointe-des-Monts?"

"Just past it, at Baie-Trinité."

"And how are you?"

"So-so."

"What's up?"

"Nothing. I just wanted to hear your voice."

There was a brief silence.

"What's the weather like on the North Shore?" she asked.

"Rainy," he said. "At Beauport?"

"The same."

"Can you still see the bridge to the island from your window?"

"Of course."

"How does it look?"

"Still beautiful and elegant."

"Thank you," he said. "Kisses."

"You too."

"On your cheek and on your eyes."

"You too," she said, lowering her voice.

He hung up. As he was getting back in the van he saw a grey-and-white cat crouched between the rear wheels.

"What are you doing there?" he said. "I've barely arrived!"

The cat disappeared into the ditch. Back at the wheel, the Driver drove the bookmobile to the old wharf to park. It was just a jetty, half-wrecked by storms, but in every village he liked to set up shop at the wharf: that way, he was sure the van was visible to everyone.

Here, though, the head of the network didn't live in the village. His job as a forest ranger required him to live further north, in a huge wildlife preserve, and he spent most of his time at the top of a tower, scanning the spruce wood in search of the first sign of a forest fire. A ham radio operator let him know when the bookmobile arrived and if the risk of fire wasn't too great, he would drive his Range Rover to the village.

With the rain he was sure to come that evening or the next day.

The Driver opened the back and put up a plastic awning to protect the children's books on the shelves fitted into the doors. He hadn't eaten since breakfast, so he fixed himself a cheese omelet and toast.

He was finishing his meal when he heard meowing under the van. He got out and bent over to have a look, shielded by the plastic: it was the grey-and-white cat he'd noticed on arriving in the village.

"You again!" he said. "I wonder if you're hungry by any chance?"

He gave the cat the remains of his omelet and went back inside.

That afternoon the rain was intensified by an offshore wind that threatened to blow away the plastic. He decided to shut the doors, but first he got the cat inside, luring him in with a bowl of milk.

"Make yourself at home," he said.

The cat inspected the van, then returned to the bowl of milk, his eyes half-closed as he lapped it up, spraying drops onto the floor. Sitting besides him with his back against the books, the Driver looked at his black notebook. The small Baie-Trinité network was recent and precarious. The books didn't circulate well because the members, mainly an Indian guide, a trapper, a biologist, and an engineer, rarely got a chance to see one another. On the other hand, because of the Indian guide the books often turned up in the baggage of wealthy tourists and travelled with them to the four corners of America.

That was precisely what the forest ranger told him when he showed up the next morning.

"There are two missing," he said, taking the books from his Range Rover. "One's gone to Louisiana, the other to Oregon."

"It doesn't matter," said the Driver.

"You don't mind?"

"On the contrary. Come in . . . Would you like a coffee?"

The rain had stopped. The cat had left at the first sight of dawn.

"Okay," said the forest ranger as he climbed into the van with his books.

The Driver poured him a coffee. One of the things he particularly liked about this man was that, unlike most readers, he often borrowed poetry. He also took nature books and novels for the members of the network, but his own tastes ran more to Quebec poetry.

He was a nervous little man, thin as a rail and prematurely worn down by cares. He'd been very active in politics, where he had experienced only disappointments, then he'd left everything – not just his work but also his wife and children – for this lonely job in the north woods. He hoped that nature would heal his wounds, physical and emotional, and to get luck on his side, he also relied on poetry.

After his coffee, the forest ranger picked out some news books, including poetry by Chamberland, Brossard, Longchamps, Charron, Francoeur, Théoret, Beaulieu, Daoust, Uguay, Delisle, Beausoleil, Miron, Desroches, Brault, and Vanier.

"This time I think I've gone overboard," he said. "Is this too many?"

"Not at all," said the Driver, smiling to reassure him.

"Why are you laughing?"

"No reason."

"Anyway, I'll try to bring them all back, every single one."

"That's fine, but don't worry about it: books are like cats, you can't always hang on to them."

"That's true."

"Aside from that, how are you?"

"Not too bad. I'm eating a little more. My stomach's better."

When he had been reassured that the forest ranger was in good shape, the Driver inquired about the other members of the network. Finally, he asked:

"Are you happy?"

He often asked the question but rare were the readers who answered it directly.

"I haven't got so many problems," replied the forest ranger.

"That's good," he said.

Soon the head of the network left with his books and the Driver was alone on the wharf, waiting for the uncertain arrival of readers. But it started to rain again and not one visitor showed up all morning, not even the grey-and-white cat.

That afternoon, a break in the weather allowed him to open the back doors again. Almost at once he saw two children arrive, the younger holding onto the other's elbow, and he recognized them despite the orange slickers that covered them completely: they came during every tour and took illustrated collections of tales or comic books. In fact each had a book under his arm, which he was bringing back.

This time the children chose *L'Espagnole et la Pékinoise*, by Gabrielle Roy, and *The Mousehole Cat*, the Driver's favorite picture book.

At the end of the evening, still comforted by their visit, he got back on the road and drove to Rivière-Pentecôte, which would be his last stop before Sept-Îles.

At Rivière-Pentecôte, he made an exception and parked the bookmobile not on the wharf but on a headland, where stood the church and, a little further away, a chapel dedicated to St. Anne. From that height he overlooked one of his favorite landscapes on the entire North Shore — one of those that he kept in his heart when he went back to the South. It was a delicately curved grassy point of land resting in the sand like a jewel in a case dividing the waters of the Rivière-Pentecôte and of the sea before they merged. That night, though, it was too dark to admire the landscape. He nibbled some cookies and went to bed.

The next morning he was wakened by cawing crows. Looking out the window, he had the impression that the headland was thinner now, but most likely that was just the effect of the incoming tide.

In this sector the head of the network was a woman who, early every morning, came to look after the chapel. She could turn up at any moment so he ate quickly. He was very surprised not to see her because you could always depend on her. He waited in vain all afternoon, greeting the village readers and some tourists, and all evening, which he spent on a bench, with his back against the wall of the chapel, gazing at the river whose water was mingling with that of the outgoing tide.

The woman didn't show up the next morning either. Or in the afternoon. He was obliged to leave and decided to drop off some books in the little chapel for her. He chose titles likely to please her and to suit her network, which was all women, and took them to leave on a prie-dieu. He was on his way back from the chapel when he saw her arrive, dressed in navy blue and carrying the books from the previous tour.

He went to meet her.

"Bonjour," he said. "We nearly missed each other."

"There's been a death in the family," she said. "My brother, the one who lived in Port-Cartier. We buried him today."

"Ah!" he said and couldn't add another word. "I . . . I'm sorry for your loss," he stammered.

"Thank you."

The woman was out of breath from climbing the hill. After going a few steps with her in silence, he told her that he'd left her some books in the chapel.

"I didn't want the women of Rivière-Pentecôte to having nothing to read."

"Thanks."

"But . . . as long as you're here, maybe you'd rather choose them yourself?"

"No, that's all right."

He put the book she was returning inside the bookmobile and followed her onto the narrow path that went up to the chapel. She went inside and knelt, but he didn't dare to copy her. Daunted, he stayed outside on the bench where he'd sat the night before to watch the river slip into the sea.

He waited for a long time. When he turned around he saw through the window that she was still kneeling on the prie-dieu next to the one on which he'd left the books. Her eyes were closed. He walked away without making a sound. His next stop was Maliotenam, a Montagnais word that means "Mary's village."

MALIOTENAM

AROUND ELEVEN O'CLOCK the next morning, the Driver drove into Sept-Îles and immediately – after crossing the river – turned right and went to the Uashat campground. Not that he intended to stay, but as it was run by Montagnais, he thought there would be a chance of finding the band there. At the gate though a guide in period costume told him that the band had come the day before, that they'd stayed all day, asking tons of questions about the Indians, and that they'd put on a show in Sept-Îles the previous night. Since they were interested in the Montagnais, they were probably at the Maliotenam reservation.

Fifteen minutes later, the Driver was at the reservation, which was only fifteen kilometers away. It was a quiet, nearly deserted village, built on sandy terrain, with modest stucco houses neatly lining the paved streets. The school bus was easily visible, parked on the main square outside a big white church with a red roof, surmounted by a steeple that looked like an odd black hood. Grouped between the bus and the church, the people from the band were checking their equipment as a dozen interested children looked on.

Leaving the bookmobile on the other side of the square, the Driver went up to them. Marie was sitting on the ground surrounded by the children, so he joined them. He rested his shoulder against hers, very gently, because she had her arms around a little girl who was snuggling between her knees.

"Bonjour!" he said softly, so as not to disturb them. "I've missed you."

"I've missed you too," she said. "Did everything go well?"

"Yes. Some days there aren't many readers, but they all have something special about them. And the network heads are very loyal."

Other children arrived, on their own or in the arms of a big sister, if they were very young. Their faces were as round as the full moon, their eyes and hair as black as coal. Around the Driver and Marie there was soon an audience of children sitting in a semicircle on the asphalt. Then a musician took out his harmonica and started to play an old tune and Mélodie, who was helping Slim to set up his high wire, began to sing:

> *While the happy, the rich and the great*
> *lie down in fine linens and silk*
> *We the outcasts, the wanderers*
> *hear lullabies lulling the stars.*

There was no applause. Not moving, their eyes shining brightly, the children waited for what would come next. One juggler picked up his balls, another his bowling pins, and they executed an act backed up by the drums. After that, Mélodie sang a second song and the band members, alternating instrumental pieces and feats of skill, presented all the parts of their show, including those with the black dog and Slim's high wire act. All through the presentation, with their usual lack of affectation, they performed as energetically as if they'd been playing to a big crowd or to distinguished guests.

In the middle of the afternoon, Marie and Mélodie went to a store on the reservation to buy groceries. The owner served them without a word, but when it came time to pay he shook his head, letting them know that the show they'd put on for the children was more than enough to pay the bill. And on his initiative, he added several boxes of tea, coffee, and tobacco.

Later, the members of the company decided to go back to Sept-Îles and the Driver went along in his bookmobile. They wanted to do some more shows there to accumulate a little money, knowing that for the last part of their journey the absence of a road would oblige them to use a costlier means of transportation.

After their show that evening, in a park across from the huge bay, its entrance guarded by the seven islands that gave the town its name, the Driver tried to find out their plans. For the time being they didn't feel like moving: the setting was magnificent, the sky cloudless and blue, the take very good. They were happy and had no plans, aside from getting up early the next morning to see the shrimp-boats come back from fishing with their escort of gulls.

"What about you?" asked Marie.

"I'm getting back on the road and I'll stop very shortly in a little place I know on the Moisie River."

"To work?"

"No, to rest and get some sun. There's a wonderful beach with sand dunes . . . Summer will soon be over and the cool weather's coming . . ."

"That sounds like a good idea to me."

She turned towards Slim and they exchanged a few words *sotto voce*. Then, speaking up as if she wanted everyone to hear:

"Can we sleep on the sand there?" she asked.

"Of course," he said.

"Then I'd love to go with you, if you don't mind."

"I don't mind in the least."

She got her sleeping bag and climbed into the bookmobile. To disguise his lack of composure, the Driver took the map and showed Slim exactly where the beach was. He advised him to be careful: if the sand was soft, vehicles were liable to get stuck, so it was best not to go past the first dune.

Before leaving Sept-Îles he stopped at a service station to fill up with gas and check the oil, because there would be fewer villages around Highway 138.

STAR DUST

THE SUN, coming after the rain, had hardened the surface of the sand so it was easy for the Driver to go beyond the first dune. He let the van coast down to the river and, to be sure of having peace, he parked at the far end of the beach.

Before eating they took off their sandals and walked in the warm sand along the river. Leaving behind them swimmers, a hydroplane hitched to a pontoon, and some people with fishing rods, they went all the way underneath the bridge. On their way back, Marie gestured to the Driver to look at the sky:

"There's an osprey," she said.

"Where?"

"He's gliding up there . . . Follow my fingertip."

"Right, now I can see him!"

Ever since she had been trying to show him birds, this was the first time he'd seen one. He enjoyed watching the osprey, awed at the ease with which it was circling above the river high in the blue sky, without even moving its wings.

"It's a bird of prey," she said. "Audubon showed it with a fish in its claws."

"How were you able to recognize it?"

"There's a kink in its wings when it flies and it's blackish above and clear white below. And I saw it dive a while ago when we got here. It dove towards the river . . . and then I lost sight of it because of the bridge."

"Maybe he's fishing for salmon: the Moisie is famous for salmon."

They were back at the bookmobile. Marie got in behind him and helped him shift the bookcases and set up the table and the folding chairs. He poured water into a saucepan, then stood at the sink for a moment studying the photo of Shakespeare and Company they both liked so much.

"I don't have anything special to offer you," he said. "Would you like some pasta?"

"I love pasta," she said.

He had spinach tortellini in tomato sauce. She ate everything on her plate and wiped up the surplus sauce with her bread. When they'd finished eating they replaced the table and chairs behind the shelves and sat on the floor across from each other to drink a cup of hot chocolate. When it was nearly dark, the Driver got up and switched on the night-light; it could attract mosquitoes so he shut the back doors.

"They've all gone," he said, taking a look outside. "All except the hydroplane."

"We'll have peace and quiet," she said.

"I like to stop here . . . There's a long love affair between the St. Lawrence and me, but sometimes this vastness, all this water stretching to infinity like a sea, tires me and I have to rest beside a small river or a lake."

"I understand."

They were sitting with their backs against the shelves, which they'd put back in place, and they were completely surrounded by books: the windows and the entrance to the cab were the only places without any.

"It's so comfortable here," said Marie. "Like a little house. We're safe, the books protect us . . . And there's a window that looks up to the sky."

He followed her gaze which was lifted towards the skylight, but it was hard to see anything because of the night-light.

"It's true that the books protect us," he said, "but their protection doesn't last forever. It's a little like dreams. One day or another, life catches up with us."

He sipped his chocolate and abruptly changed the subject.

"So," he said, "if I've understood correctly your friends don't intend to stop when the road ends. They want to go on by boat and visit the little villages all the way to Blanc-Sablon?"

"Yes," she said. "They want to take the *Nordik Express*, but they don't know if they'll have enough money."

"Anyway, they're right to want to go there: the landscapes are more spectacular than anything you've seen till now."

"Is it wilder?"

"Yes. The trees are stunted, there's a lot of granite. Wait a minute . . ."

Setting his cup of chocolate on the floor he got up and, without having to look for it, took a book from a shelf. It was the journal of Jacques Cartier. He stood under the night-light, turned a few pages and read the following passage:

"This entire coast contains not one barrow-load of good soil. There are only jagged rocks: by way of vegetation, only moss, and as for trees, only runts. Truly, if one considers it, one might conclude that it is the land God gave to Cain."

"He didn't think much of it," Marie observed.

"No, he didn't. For him, the lack of greenery made for a bleak landscape . . . But actually there are colors everywhere: pink granite, green and orange lichen, white and red flowers dotting the moss. And you'll see, the villages are pretty and the people are very friendly."

He returned the book to the shelf and came back to sit across from Marie.

She explained: "I'd love to go there, for the reasons you gave and also to see certain birds – razor-billed auks, puffins, loons – but I don't know if I'll have time. I have to go back to Quebec City soon if I don't want to miss my plane."

She took a long sip of chocolate and then, in an unsteady voice and without looking at him:

"Do you stop at Havre-Saint-Pierre?"

"Yes," he said, "but I may go back to Quebec City to submit my report to the Ministry."

"Oh yes?"

"You could come to Quebec with me if you want. I usually go by way of the Gaspé Peninsula."

"I'll have to think about it," she said. "Thanks very much."

She heaved a long sigh. He saw a shadow leave her face: a kind of black bird that beat its wing and flew away.

"Are you all right?" he asked.

"Yes. A little better."

"Not too sleepy?"

"No. Why?"

"I'd like you to tell me about your work, how you go about it, okay?"

"I'll try."

She collected her thoughts for a moment, then recited: "Ultra-marine . . . yellow ochre . . . titanium white . . . burnt Sienna . . . red madder . . . burnt umber . . . The names are beautiful, aren't they?"

"Very."

"That was for atmosphere . . . Now, let's say that I want to paint an osprey: first I have to find his nest and observe him through my binoculars. I note everything I see – his white belly, his long angled wings which are also white but with black spots, the distance between his eye and his hooked bill, the way he flies and dives – and I make sketches. After that I go home to . . ."

". . . feed the cats."

"Yes," she said smiling. "And also to think about a problem that's beginning to worry me."

"What's that?"

"I have to find a setting for my osprey. Instead of painting him all alone I want to incorporate him into a landscape that will show him off to advantage. But I haven't been able to think up that landscape. I look all over when I'm walking, but I can't come up with it. So I give up . . . And then one day at the seashore, I'm walking along a path that leads to a rocky cliff, when all at once I'm surrounded by a light fog. That cliff in the fog just ahead of me is exactly the landscape I've been looking for!"

"Bravo!" he said.

She paused and finished her chocolate.

"So now what do you do?" he asked.

"I study all the details and let them seep into my memory, then I go home to . . ."

". . . paint a picture?"

"Not right away. First I make a big drawing with all the elements of the landscape: the conifers, the deciduous trees, the cliff, the rocks, and the sea with its patches of fog. Then I sketch the osprey on tracing paper and slowly move it over the big drawing to look for the place that suits it best. When I've found it, I'm ready to start my painting."

She fell silent. The presentation was over.

"Thank you," he said. "It was very nice of you to tell me all that."

"You're very welcome."

"Would you like some more chocolate? Some LU cookies?"

"No," she said.

"What would you like?"

"I'm a little sleepy . . . I think I'll go to bed soon."

She stifled a yawn.

While he was looking at her he noticed beside her head a book he was very fond of – *Star Dust*, by Hubert Reeves. Even in the half-light he could identify books by certain details: a patch of color, a symbol, the size of the title. He got up, moved the shelving unit, and turned his back to Marie as he put her cup in the sink.

"Can I sleep with you?" he asked.

"Sure," she said.

"Have you got anything to protect you from the mosquitoes and blackflies?"

"No."

He went to the cab and rummaged in the glove compartment, then came back with a bottle of citronella. Marie was still hugging her knees. He knelt beside her and opened the bottle.

"Smells good," she said.

He poured a few drops onto his fingertips and, while she closed her eyes, he patted it all over her face, with special attention to her cheekbones; then he added a bit to her neck and behind her ears. After that she took the bottle and returned the favor. Surrounded by the scent of citronella they climbed out of the van with their sleeping bags, spread them side-by-side on the sand, took off their shoes and got inside. It wasn't very warm so they pulled the zippers up to their faces.

A murmur of water and insects came from the river but they got used to it and finally didn't even hear it. When the heat of their bodies had warmed the inside of the sleeping bags, they pulled off their jeans and rolled them up to make pillows. Then they began to look at the stars.

The Driver's knowledge was limited to the Big Dipper, the Little Dipper, and two or three constellations nearby, so she showed him how to find the Dolphin by following the long path from one star to another, beginning at the pole star. He traced the path several times to be sure that he knew it by heart.

"Thank you," he said.

After a brief silence he turned to her.

"Are you asleep?" he murmured.

"No," she said faintly. "What are you thinking about?"

"About Hubert Reeves's books. Have you read them?"

"Not all of them," she said. "But I know his ideas a little. We are the children of the universe . . . We live on a planet that's lost in space . . . We're made out of star dust. Is that what you were thinking about?"

"Yes. It's very impressive, very beautiful even, but . . ."

"But what?"

"I don't feel the connection, the filiation he talks about. I mean, I don't have the feeling that I'm part of a whole. Actually, I feel totally isolated, all alone . . . What about you?"

She thought it over for a few moments.

"It seems to me," she said, "that I'm part of a kind of chain. Like in your networks of readers."

He tried to see if she was serious or not, but she'd buried her face in her sleeping bag. Reaching out his arm, he furtively brushed the curly grey hair that protruded.

RIVIÈRE-AU-TONNERRE

WHEN THE SCHOOL BUS came into sight at the top of the dune, the Driver said goodbye to Marie and then to the people in the band and got back on the road by himself.

Grappling with dark ideas, he drove abstractedly along a nearby deserted road where villages were rare. Now the spruce trees on the flanks of the hills were smaller. The sea, its color a dark blue verging on violet, stretched out as far as the eye could see. An hour later he stopped at the falls on the Manitou River to stretch his legs and have a coffee. After that, having assured himself that there were no cats under the van, he got back in and drove to the village of Rivière-au-Tonnerre, the second-to-last stop on his tour.

When he got to the wharf around noon, the tide was low and the sun had lost some of its ardor, but it still felt warm on his skin. After a quick bite to eat he went out to walk on the beach, leaving the bookmobile open and a note saying: "Come in and make yourself at home. Back soon. The Driver." He walked down a slope covered with beach peas, went around some mossy rocks, and when he reached the place where the sand was soft underfoot, he took off his sandals and slowly continued on his way. Now and then he turned around to see if any readers had arrived.

The head of the network was a fisherman's wife. She worked part-time in a fish processing plant. The Driver didn't know exactly what her work consisted of: the first time she'd mentioned the plant, he had understood that the fish was made into cat food and he preferred to leave it at that.

In recent years the network had been giving him cause for concern. The fisherman's wife was liable to be forced to move. It was harder and harder for her husband to earn anything from cod-fishing, because of competition from the big trawlers. They were considering a move to Havre-Saint-Pierre, a town where fishermen could get work taking tourists to visit the Mingan islands.

At the end of the bay the Driver turned again to look at the wharf. As far as he could judge from this distance, there were no readers. He rested for a minute, then made his way along the sandbar, looking for the rock he visited during every tour. He spotted it in the distance. In appearance there was nothing special about the rock except perhaps its location, far from any others, and the fact that it listed to the left. But as he got closer he easily found what he was looking for: in a crevice that made you think of a shoulder there was a miniature garden, with a carpet of moss, a freshwater pool, some lichen, and one blue iris.

That afternoon some tourists in a Winnebago stopped near the bookmobile. They were looking for maps and leaflets about the villages on the Lower North Shore. The Driver only had a few for his own use but he gave them an address in Havre-Saint-Pierre where they could get what they wanted. Just as they were leaving, the fisherman's wife arrived on her bike, a pile of books tied up with string on the rack. A pleasant chubby woman in her forties, she had on overalls, a checked shirt with the sleeves rolled up, and knee-high rubber boots.

"How are you doing?" asked the Driver.

"Very well," she said. "What about you?"

"Not bad."

He got out of the van to shake hands. Hers were bigger than his and she had red cheeks and little creases around her eyes. Every time he saw her, he had the impression that he was looking at her husband, though he'd never met him.

He helped her untie the string around the books.

"How's the fishing?" he asked. "Any improvement?"

"Some," she said. "My husband's started fishing for scallops and snow crab. But it's not like the cod-fishing used to be . . ."

"That goes without saying," he said.

She handed him the pile of books and went inside the bookmobile. Sitting in the doorway with the books beside him and his feet dangling, he inquired about some of the others in the network. Then he was quiet and let her choose her books.

After she left there were visits from some individual readers. The next day there were a few more. Late in the afternoon, when he wasn't expecting anyone else, a young girl with a backpack arrived: Simone. Though she was only about twenty he considered her to be one of the biggest readers on the whole North Shore. It wasn't enough for her to be part of the network run by the fisherman's wife, she needed to pick out her own books too.

She climbed nimbly into the van and emptied her bag onto the folding table. It contained fourteen books, all works of fiction.

"There's one missing," she said.

Slim and vivacious with big brown eyes, she was wearing a very short flowered dress. A faint perfume drifted around her.

"That's all right," he said.

"It's *White Fang*, by Jack London. I lent it to a friend and she's gone to Dawson in the Yukon. I don't even know if she'll come back."

"I hope you'll see your friend again, but don't worry about the book: I have another copy."

"So it's not too serious?"

"Not at all."

As casually as he could, he asked:

"Do you often lend books?"

"Fairly often," she said. "Is that bad?"

"On the contrary, it's very good. Really very good."

"That's a relief! I was scared!"

She spun around, making the hem of her flowered dress swirl, and began to look at the books on the shelves. As she usually asked him for advice, he stayed in the library with her. He offered her some books, she took them in her long, sinewy hands, paged through them briefly and decided very quickly whether to take them or not.

When he saw that she'd nearly finished he left her for a moment and went into the cab. Taking the black notebook from the glove compartment, he opened it to the page for Rivière-au-Tonnerre and noted for his successor that should the fisherman's wife move to Havre-Saint-Pierre, young Simone had the necessary qualities to replace her.

He jumped when she stuck her head inside the cab.

"Excuse me," she said.

"Yes?" he said. Briskly, he closed the notebook.

"I've finished . . . Could I have a manuscript?"

"Of course."

After he'd put back the notebook he went behind the seat to open the chest full of rejected manuscripts. He was nervous and made a mistake, opening the chest that held his tools and the length of flexible tubing. He shut it at once, muttering an apology, and hastened to open the other chest. Then he left her and went back to the bookcase.

The books that she wanted to take were piled on the table next to those she'd brought back. As the Driver had made a good many suggestions, most of the books she'd chosen were favorites of his, books that had illuminated his life in the same way that lighthouses guide the sailors on the river. The pile included *The Old Man and the Sea*, *The Catcher in the Rye*, *L'Éclum des jours*, *L'Avalée des avalés*, *The World According to Garp*, *Salut Galarneau!*, *Le Grand Meaulnes*, *On the Road*, *Agaguk*, *Bonjour tristesse*, and *Letters to a Young Poet*. He also spotted *La Storia* by Elsa Morante, *Les Bons Sentiments*, *The Bleeding Heart* by Marilyn French, short stories by André Major, and *The Heart Is a Lonely Hunter* by Carson McCullers. In all, once again she had around fifteen titles.

The young girl came back from the cab with two manuscripts.

"Will you help me choose?" she asked.

"You don't have to," he said. "Take them both."

"That's really nice of you. Thanks a lot."

Without wasting a minute she stowed the books and manuscripts in her pack and climbed out of the van. He followed her and helped her hoist the pack onto her back.

"Thanks," she said. "See you next time!"

"Enjoy them!"

She left, giving him a timid smile. He sat on the running board and watched her walk away in the sunlight. With her very short flowered dress and her backpack bulging with books, she was the very image of life. He kept watching her for a long time and his eyes misted over when she disappeared behind the first house in the village.

THE END OF THE ROAD

H E GOT TO Havre-Sainte-Pierre around seven o'clock in the evening, in weather that was cool and foggy. In the hope of seeing Maric again he went directly to the port, covering it slowly from one end to the other, but the school bus was nowhere to be seen. He got out to buy a sandwich and fries from a trailer that bore the name *Roi de la patate*. The man working there hadn't seen the people from the band. Chatting with him, the Driver found out that the coolness of the air was due to the presence of a number of icebergs that had entered the Gulf and were drifting along the coast.

After he'd eaten he drove through the little town to the municipal campground. At the office, the guard said that he hadn't seen the bus and that in any case, the campground had been full for several days now. So he drove back to the port, found a parking spot and went to bed early.

There was no readers' network in Havre-Saint-Pierre, but the Driver had become friendly with the hydroplane pilot who conveyed travelers and goods to several spots along the Lower North

Shore. When the weather was fine the pilot took books in his baggage hold and distributed them on his own to readers he knew in the different villages. He worked for the Aérogolfe company, whose offices were on a lake behind the town the people called "the airplane lake."

When he woke up the next morning he was glad to see that though it was still cool, a westerly wind had driven away the fog and scattered the clouds. As soon as he was dressed he went to the lake. Despite the early hour a number of cars were already parked behind the trailer that housed the airline company. The Driver recognized the pilot's old Oldsmobile. The converging lines of the hood always reminded him of a sentence he was fond of from Réjean Ducharme's novel *Dévadé*: "There was a suggestion of shark, of killer whale, in the gleaming black hood, in the horizontal swoop of the Oldsmobile that burst through the luxury of the snow transfigured by orange light from the streetlamps."

His friend's hydroplane, a dark yellow Beaver with a red line down the length of the fuselage, was parked next to a wooden pontoon on which half a dozen people in brightly colored warm clothes were sitting on their baggage, waiting.

As he drove behind the trailer, the Driver tapped his horn and the pilot's face appeared at the window; he'd be there as soon as he had finished his paperwork. To get a better view of the lake the Driver backed up, then he opened the two rear doors.

When he was downing his cornflakes he heard the feeble sound of an engine. A black dot appeared on the horizon and steadily expanded, then the sound grew louder and a blue-and-white Cessna touched down in the middle of the lake. As it came near the shore, the aircraft described a broad curve on the water and then, with its engine cut, glided slowly to the pontoon next to the one to which the Beaver was secured. Out of it stepped three men who, judging by their get-up, were returning from a fishing trip. The men loaded their baggage into a van, and when they had gone the lake was quiet again. A few sounds could be heard – scraps of conversation between the Beaver's passengers, the clink of tools the mechanic was using for a repair – but they didn't disturb the tranquility of this nearly circular little lake with no trees around it, that was lost in an expanse of blueberries and Labrador tea.

The Driver washed his dishes and made coffee for two. He had just poured himself a cup when the pilot arrived, carrying a big box of books.

"Smells good!' he said.

"Bonjour!" said the Driver. "Would you like a cup?"

"Would I ever! Thanks!"

Setting the box on the floor of the van, the pilot scrambled inside. He was a tall man with a thin blonde moustache and he wore his hair smoothed back. In his cracked leather jacket and his white silk scarf he reminded one of aviators like Saint-Exupérty or Mermoz or some other pilot of the Aéropostale with the mission of going to Buenos Aires, flying over the South Atlantic at night.

He accepted the cup the Driver was holding out and took several sips right away.

"That does a man good!" he said. "How was your trip?"

"Very fine."

"So the old engine's still holding up?"

"Oh yes," said the Driver. He winced, as if the pilot were talking about his own age, not the bookmobile's. Without letting his concern show, he started taking books from the box and piling them on the table.

The pilot leaned outside to keep an eye on the mechanic who was bustling around the engine of the hydroplane.

"There's nothing like an old carcass," he said.

It was hard to guess the age of this cheerful and spirited man whose life had always been filled with adventure. He'd spent a number of years flying water-bombers in the south of France, near Marseille, to battle the forest fires that broke out in periods of drought.

He started choosing books. As he was thinking out loud you could see that he had specific readers in mind when he made his choices: the general storekeeper in Natashquan, a Montagnais guide in La Romaine, a woman in an old folks' home at Harrington Harbor, a man who worked at a boat factory in Saint-Augustin, a nurse at the hospital in Blanc-Sablon . . .

As he selected books, the Driver placed them in the cardboard carton. When it was nearly full he alerted the pilot, who took another two or three novels.

"That's it," he said. "I think I've got something for everybody."

"If you want more we can make another parcel," said the Driver.

"No, this will be fine. Thanks anyway."

"I should be thanking you: you extend my work. Thanks to you my books get to isolated villages and they warm people's spirits."

"I'm glad to do it," said the pilot. He put the last books in the box himself, then he shut it up, interweaving the flaps.

"What about you," he asked, "are you going directly back to Quebec City?"

"I'll spend a day or two here," said the Driver. "I didn't travel on my own this time, I was with friends . . . They should be here soon."

He told the pilot about meeting the people in the band and about the journey they'd made with him, stopping to put on their shows.

"And now," he added, "they want to take the *Nordik Express* to the villages on the Lower North Shore, provided they can come up with the money . . ."

"The cheapest way to travel is by boat," said the pilot. "And if they don't have the full amount they can always stop in a village and get the boat again on its way back."

"You're right, I hadn't thought of that."

There was a sound of footsteps and the mechanic appeared at the back of the bookmobile.

"I've filled her up and everything's in order," he said.

"Thanks," said the pilot. "Would you ask the passengers to take their seat? . . . I'll be along in a minute."

While the mechanic was on his way back to the hydroplane, the Driver craned his neck to look at the sky. The clouds were few and very high.

"You'll have fine weather," he said.

"Yes," said the pilot. "Not very warm, but at least there won't be any fog." He touched the table, which was wood. Then he asked abruptly: "Why don't you take the boat with your friends?"

"Well, because . . . they aren't all going."

"Oh no?"

"No. There's a woman . . . She has to go back to France for her work. Her plane leaves from Quebec City so . . ."

"So you're taking her there."

"Yes."

"By way of the Gaspé?"

The Driver smiled without replying. There was a hint of sadness in his smile, but the pilot wasn't aware of it.

"What's this woman like?" he asked.

"She's . . . she's special. Her name is Marie."

"And are . . ." he began, then stopped. "I'd better go before I say something stupid," he concluded and picked up the carton of books. At the bottom of the steps he turned around.

"See you next time!" he said.

"Keep well!" said the Driver.

"Have a good trip!"

"You too!"

"Good luck with Marie!"

With his white scarf drifting over his shoulder, the pilot made his way to the plane. He stowed the books in the hold and carefully fastened the panel. Once he was in the cockpit he donned sunglasses and, as he always did, gave a thumbs-up salute to the Driver. The propeller began to turn with a throbbing that made the old bookmobile shudder on the shore, then slowly the hydroplane moved away on its floats. The pilot picked up speed, took off and banked.

SAYING GOODBYE TO THE BAND

THE *Nordik Express* was getting ready to leave. On the wharf, Slim was holding Marie in his arms and murmuring something in her ear.

She was shorter than he was; her head was on his shoulder, her eyes were half-closed and she was listening intently. A moment later she freed herself gently and began to say something in turn; she had one finger raised and seemed to be giving him some advice, but each of her moves ended with her stroking his cheek or his hair.

Ignoring them, the other members of the band were checking their baggage one last time before boarding the red-and-white ship. The Driver stood off to the side and, along with some other passengers, watched the boat's crane lift cartons, containers and even automobiles off the wharf, then set them down with great precision on the afterdeck. Now and then he cast a worried glance at Slim and Marie.

The band had now been at Havre-Saint-Pierre for two days. While they were in Sept-Îles the weather had deteriorated, so they hadn't been able to collect the money they needed to take the boat. But when they'd arrived, they'd performed in the port next to the shipping company's offices, and one of its representatives who had liked the show had offered them a free round-trip if they'd be willing to give a few performances to entertain the passengers. They'd accepted. Marie had announced that she wasn't going with them.

When a siren gave the signal to embark, the Driver joined the musicians, wished them a good trip and good luck, and petted the black dog one last time. Next to him, Marie also made her goodbyes to everyone and he heard her ask one of them if he had enough warm clothes, another if he'd remembered to bring his camera, and Mélodie if she had her turtleneck sweater and her honey throat lozenges. While she spoke she would clasp a hand, touch a cheek, hug a shoulder, pick a thread off a jacket.

One by one the musicians got on board with their baggage until finally the only ones left at the foot of the gangplank were the acrobat, the singer, Marie, and the Driver. No doubt there was a silent question in Marie's eyes because Slim took her by the arm and said firmly: "Don't worry about it!" She turned to Mélodie then, kissed her cheeks and hugged her for a long time. The singer and Slim joined their friends, who had already settled in on the upper deck.

The moorings were cast off and the *Nordik Express* left the harbor, stirring up eddies of foam. On the wharf, the Driver and Marie waved goodbye as long as they could see the hands waving on the deck; when they thought it was finished, there was still one hand waving in the distance. Finally, the boat disappeared on the horizon and they began to shiver in the chilly air. It was barely eight a.m.

"Should we make coffee?" the Driver suggested.

"Good idea," said Marie. "But you'll be my guest because the school bus is still here."

They climbed into the bus, which was parked beside a shed, and sat on the seats in the "parlor." Articles of clothing were lying around here and there and the table was cluttered with the dishes that the others had used when making their lunches. Long before the coffee was ready they were warm from the sunlight reflected off the tin walls of the shed.

When they'd finished their coffee they tidied up and Marie removed all the perishables from the fridge. She gathered up her things, drew the curtains and, before leaving, looked around the inside of the bus.

"You can stay for a while," said the Driver, "we're in no hurry. Take your time . . ."

She shrugged and seemed to hesitate. He added:

"I'll get gas and groceries, then I'll come back for you. How does that sound?"

"It's kind of you, but it's not necessary. I'll just write them a note: that will be a little warmth for them when they come back."

"All right. Shall I leave now and you'll join me later?"

"No . . . Stay!" A very soft light came on in her grey-blue eyes. "Please, stay," she said.

Without a word, he sat down across from her. From her baggage she took a pen and a notebook, tore out a squared sheet and wrote: "Half of my heart is with you. Marie." He had no trouble reading it upside down. She placed it under an ashtray in the middle of the table. He got up first to operate one last time the compressed air system that opened the door and they got out, bringing the baggage and the bag of food. As arranged with Slim, they locked the doors and left the key at the *Roi de la palate*.

When they got to the bookmobile, two young tabby cats were waiting. Marie put the food in the fridge and poured milk into a soup dish for the cats. The Driver studied the road map to calculate how long it would take them to get to Quebec City by way of the Gaspé, then he came back to Marie who as usual was sitting with her back against the books. That was the position in which she felt most comfortable, as if the books gave her energy, but that morning her face looked drawn and her head was swaying slightly from side to side.

"Something wrong?" he asked.

"Nothing serious," she said. "I'm worried about Slim."

She didn't want to say anything more. Gradually her face relaxed and she managed to smile faintly. He sat down beside her, holding his map; she put on her glasses and he outlined their route with his index finger: they would retrace their steps as far as Godbout, cross

· 152 ·

the river and drive along the South Shore, making a long loop that would bring them back to Quebec City.

"Do we have time to do all that?" she asked.

"Yes, of course," he said. "If you like, we can even rest for a while before we leave."

"What about you, who do you feel like doing? Do you want to go right away?"

He tried to fold up the map but his hand was shaking a little and it took several tries.

"I don't really know what I want," he said. "Everything that used to be clear is complicated now . . . Will you do something for me?"

"Of course."

"Please stretch out your legs."

She complied. He lay down on his side with his head on her jeans, just above her knees.

"I'd like to stay like this for a minute," he said, closing his eyes.

THE BELLY OF THE WHALE

T HEY HAD SAID that they weren't in a hurry but when they left Havre-Saint-Pierre, something they had no control over impelled them to drive faster than usual. Taking turns at the wheel, they only stopped once, in Sept-Îles for a bite to eat, and it wasn't six o'clock yet when they arrived in Godbout.

But the last boat had left. They'd have to wait till morning, or go on to Baie-Comeau where there was a night crossing. They decided to stay and parked their vehicle facing the river, in the farthest corner of the pier, then got out.

The sun had disappeared behind the hills. It was the first week of September, summer was ending, and already spots of yellow and red were brightening the background of dark green spruce trees.

"Did you see the colors?" asked Marie.

"Of course," said the Driver. "But wait till we're closer to Quebec City; it will be even more beautiful."

"Because of the maples?"

"Yes. Autumn's coming . . ."

The words hung there. He'd have given anything to take them back but that was impossible.

"I'm a little chilly," said Marie.

"You didn't eat much," he said. "We should get some chocolate bars or something . . . I see a dispenser over there."

He jerked his head in the direction of a building across from the pier where passengers could take shelter. Inside they found two dispensers, one with chocolate and candy, the other with coffee; there were also restrooms, a telephone and a small waiting room with a window that looked out on the river. They separated to visit the bathroom.

The Driver came back to the waiting room first and he spied, standing with his back to him and looking out the window, the tall silhouette of his father; he had on his old raincoat and his grey fedora with the little feather, and his white hair fell in waves down his neck. A few seconds later the man turned around; needless to say, it wasn't his father.

Marie joined him while he was looking at the candy dispenser. He asked what she wanted.

"Whatever you're having," she said.

"That means a KitKat."

He fed coins into the machine and took out the bars.

"Coffee too?"

"Not right now."

The waiting room was empty. Through the window, they could make out the white spot of the ferry becoming blurred in the distance on the river, in a spot still bathed in sunlight.

"I saw my father just now," he said.

"You did?"

"I see him more and more often. Most of the time he turns his back and looks out at the river. Once he just stood there on the steps of a church. The doors were open and he was looking inside."

Marie listened patiently without taking her eyes off the last rays of sunlight on the river. When he fell silent, she said:

"With me, it's my daughter. Sometimes she's walking on the sidewalk ahead of me so I can catch up with her, but then it's someone else. Or I see her in the distance, she's talking with friends and I go up to her but . . ."

"I didn't know you had a daughter," he said.

"Yes," she said. "She has a special place in my heart."

He smiled when she said that. She asked why.

"An image came to me," he said. "Is your heart divided into several rooms, like a house? Is one of them a little bedroom with flowered wallpaper and muslin curtains and a teddy bear on a dresser?"

"I don't know," she said, laughing at his description. "Anyway, she's a big girl now. She does very well on her own."

"Are you married then?"

"No."

"I'm sorry," he said. "I won't ask any more indiscreet questions."

"It's all right," she said very softly.

Looking contrite, he went back to the dispensers and returned with two cups of coffee.

"Careful, it's hot!"

"Thanks."

She took little sips, then sat down in front of the window.

"I wonder where they are now," she said.

"Your friends?"

"Yes."

He sat down beside her, looked at his watch, and thought for a moment.

"They'll be at Natashquan soon."

"Already?"

"If you want you can phone them . . . There's a leaflet in the glove compartment that gives arrival times in the different villages and it would be easy to get the number of a place where tourists are likely to go – the general store or a restaurant . . ."

Their conversation was interrupted now and then by the hissing air brakes of a tow truck driving onto the pier and settling in for the night; invariably, during the minute that followed, someone would come into the waiting room and head for the restrooms.

Marie sipped some coffee, then balanced the cup on her knee.

"It's reassuring to know that I can get in touch," she said. "Thank you so much. I'll call later; for the time being it's best to leave them in peace. Anyway, I know they can manage perfectly well."

Her voice, in contrast with her words, was unsteady. The Driver couldn't help keeping an eye on the coffee cup whose balance was threatened whenever Marie gestured as she spoke or turned her head to look at the people coming into the room. He said: "The simplest thing would be to call when they're back at Havre-Saint-Pierre. I've got the shipping company's number in my leaflets."

"That's great," she said. She picked up her cup and drained the rest of the coffee. "I'm warmed up now. How about you?"

"Me too."

"Let's walk for a while before it's pitch black."

They went out. Strangely it wasn't as dark as they'd imagined from inside and the streetlamps weren't on yet. As they walked back and forth along the wharf where several big trucks were parked in a row, they talked about things and people they knew: the band, cats, the Driver's sister, Shakespeare and Company, Marie's parents, birds; finally, they talked about Jack.

"He should be back in Cap-Rouge now," said the Driver.

"I hope his new book is taking shape," said Marie. She thought for a moment, then added: "When I think about his book I always imagine a baby in its mother's womb. He'd probably laugh if he heard that . . ."

"I don't think he would, but he'd certainly say that he can't write a book in nine months: he needs four or five years when everything's going well."

"Why?"

"I don't know. When I first started making these rounds I'd often go to see him and ask questions. I wanted to know how books come into the world . . . And it's still a mystery to me. The older we get, the fewer certainties we have."

Marie made no reply. They walked along the line of trucks in silence for a few moments and suddenly, he began to shake his head as if a serious discussion were going on inside him.

"That business about getting old," he said, "I didn't want to talk about it but since I brought it up . . . There are a couple of things I have to say, to explain. And then I won't talk about it anymore."

She let him know that she was ready to listen.

"I'm not sick," he said. "My health is neither good nor bad, it's acceptable. As far as age is concerned, I'm no longer young but I'm not an old man either. Still, I've lived long enough to know that everything people say about our golden years, wisdom, serenity – that's all totally false. At my age I haven't learned any of the essential things – the meaning of life, good and evil . . . It's as if all my experience boils down to nothing. I'm exaggerating, but not much, I swear. Even worse, I still have the same fears, the same desires, the same needs that I had as a child. When the physical problems come along – and they're inevitable – it will be disaster, ruin. That's what

I don't want to live through. It doesn't interest me. And that's that, I won't talk about it ever again."

In spite of himself he was worked up and his tone had hardened. By way of apology, he said: "I bet the streetlamps will be on before we get back."

"What do you bet?" she asked.

They were at the far end of the wharf, near the pier.

"A dish of spaghetti."

"You're on!"

Walking normally, they got to the bookmobile and had time to go back and forth three times before the lights came on. The Driver cooked the spaghetti. After they'd eaten they sat on the floor with their backs against the books and chatted and sipped hot chocolate in the glow of the night-light. Time was now passing more slowly. Because of her fatigue, every so often Marie's head would slump onto her shoulder and he noticed behind her one of his very favorite books, *Enchantment and Sorrow*. The name of the author, Gabrielle Roy, was printed on the front cover in mauve, like the fireweed they'd seen all over along the North Shore.

Quebec books weren't in a special place in the bookcase, they were mixed in with the others, so that side by side were the books of Anne Hébert and Hemingway, Raymond Carver and Roch Carrier, Boris Vian and Gilles Vigneault, Pierre Morency and Patrick Modiano, David Goodis and Jacques Godbout, Le Clézio and Félix Leclerc.

Marie couldn't suppress a yawn, half-concealing it with the back of her hand. Automatically he yawned too, which made them both laugh.

"I'm ready to drop," she said.

"We drove too much today," he said. "Tomorrow we'll stop more often, all right?"

"Yes. I'm sorry, I have to go back to the waiting room."

"So do I."

They took their toilet kits and went outside, weaving between the trucks that were more and more numerous. In the waiting room, men and women were drinking coffee and talking about the high cost of living. The Driver, who'd finished first, went outside to wait for Marie. The pink glow from the street lamps kept them from seeing the stars.

When they got back it was a little chilly inside the bookmobile because the skylight was open. The Driver closed it and then, to warm up the room, he burned some alcohol in a tin can that he'd put in a larger can as precaution. He pushed the shelving unit along its rail and Marie helped him open up his bed. Then he helped her unroll her sleeping bag onto an air mattress beside it. They closed the curtains on the back doors and the cab, then the Driver switched off the night-light. When he started to pull off his clothes, she did too, then they lay down, each in their own bed. The alcohol burned with a blue flame, light and shimmering.

"Are you cold?" he asked.

"No," she said. Still, she pulled up the zipper of her sleeping bag.

"Are you ready to sleep?"

"Yes. You?"

"Me too. But if you can't get to sleep or if you're cold or if you need anything . . . You understand?"

"Yes. And the same goes for you." Her voice was already heavy with sleep.

"Goodnight," he said.

"Goodnight."

The alcohol burned for twenty minutes or so, casting moving shadows on the rows of books, but Marie fell asleep long before that. Half-sitting, the Driver could see that she had turned to face him, with her knees pulled up inside her sleeping bag, her face serene and eyes closed. Her breathing was deep and regular.

He tried to match her rhythm, but it didn't help him get to sleep. He turned onto his back and stayed in that position for a long time, with his eyes wide open, then he turned to face the books. If he reached out his hand he could touch them. An hour or so later he sat up in bed and silently got into his sweater and jeans. Barefoot on the cold floor, he stepped over the tin of alcohol that had finished burning and got in the cab to put on his tennis shoes. Then he went out, closing the door as quietly as he could.

It was a peaceful night. The lights were out in the cabs of the trucks and there was no one in the waiting room on the pier. He looked out the window at the river but he had to press his nose against the glass and there wasn't much to see anyway. He stood at the dispensers for a moment, checking out the different kinds of chocolate bars, chewing gum, chips and candy. He glanced indiscreetly inside the women's room, then went outside to walk. His shoes didn't make a sound.

He lowered the window a little to muffle the slamming of the door when he got back inside the bookmobile. Inside her sleeping bag, Marie stirred but didn't wake up. After he'd taken off his clothes he lay down and this time he felt sleep creeping over him.

When the roar of engines woke him abruptly, he thought that he'd barely fallen asleep. Marie, sitting up on her little bed, had also been startled awake. Before even looking outside they realized that the ferry was in and the first trucks were boarding. They dressed quickly and folded up both beds, and he drove into one of the lines of vehicles.

The ferry was a huge blue-and-white vessel called the *Camille-Marcoux*. The entire front end was open, exposing its entrails, and as he drove his van into that gaping mouth the Driver felt as if he were rushing into the belly of a whale.

THE DOG IN THE SIDECAR

The sky was clouding over when they disembarked at Matane, on the South Shore. Turning their backs on Quebec City, they drove onto Highway 132, en route for the Gaspé Peninsula, and this time they didn't hurry. They had six days until Marie's departure.

Traffic was heavier now and the villages closer together, but the river hadn't changed: it was still just as broad, patient and majestic, and Marie looked at it, dazzled.

"There'll be a big void when it's not there anymore," she said. "I don't know if I'll be able to get used to it."

"That reminds me of something," he said. "When I went to France, I lived in three places in particular: Paris, Tournon, and Le Verdon-sur-Mer . . . But I already told you that, didn't I?"

"Yes."

"Well, I realized when I came home that in each case, without doing it deliberately, I'd gone to a place on a river: the Seine, the Rhône, and the Gironde."

"The Gironde . . ." she murmured, "I don't know it very well. Isn't there a song about it by Yves Montand?"

"Yes, there is. Wait a minute . . ."

He glanced in the rear-view mirror, cleared his throat and began to sing softly:

"*L'eau de la Gironde . . . fait le tour du mond . . . quand tu me prends la main* . . . I forget the title," he added. "Do you like Yves Montand?"

"Of course."

"Me too. It was terrible when he died . . . He sang the very first song I heard on a record, at my grandfather's house when I was a child: 'The Song of the Partisans.' Do you know it?"

"Yes."

"I remember, the lyrics frightened me but at the same time they attracted me."

They stopped in Cap-Chat to buy groceries and go to the post office, because Marie wanted to buy stamps. It wasn't noon yet but they were hungry and decided to prepare a meal right there in the parking lot. Then they walked down the main street for a while, looking into the store windows. In the distance, towards the west, against a grey sky, they spotted a tall white windmill that reminded them of the mast of a sailboat. Before getting back in the bookmobile they bent down to check between the wheels, but there weren't any cats.

Marie drove. She asked him to go on recalling his memories. "It's good for me to hear them," she said.

"Would you like to hear a little story about ducks?"

"Sure."

"When I was at Le Verdon, on the south shore of the Gironde, to save money I stayed away from campsites. I had an understanding with the police: at night they'd leave me alone on condition that I park my old bus at the end of the beach or across from the little sea port. There was nothing as beautiful as the fine sand beach that stretched all to the horizon, but I preferred the sea port with its fishing boats and its tidy rows of sailboats in the basin and its forest of masts and the clinking sound of steel cables as they swayed and its family of ducks."

"What kind of ducks?"

"They had dark green heads and the rest of the body was grey or brown."

"With a white ring around the neck?"

"I didn't notice."

"They were probably mallards or shovelers. Did they have yellow bills?"

"I don't know. Even though I watched them for hours. At certain times, depending on the angle of the light, the green of their heads suddenly turned dark blue. But what interested me most was the floating house that the people at the yacht club had put up for them in a quiet part of the basin. It was made of wood and sat on a kind of raft with two oil drums for floats and it was fastened to the shore by a fairly long rope so it could move with the tides. Every day a member of the club would go to the basin, pull the rope and leave some food at the door of the house. And on the road that went around the harbor there were signs reading 'Duck Crossing,' to urge drivers to slow down."

While he was recounting these stories the landscape had changed. The narrow paved road was now squeezed in between the sea and a hill that was getting steeper and steeper. The tide was out and Marie was driving very slowly so as not to lose sight of the sometimes strange rocky formations that bristled from the sandbar. At L'Anse-Pleureuse they drove off Highway 132 and went to a rest stop along a river, on the road to Murdochville. They chose the picnic table closest to an embankment covered with closely mown grass that sloped gently down towards a lake; it was just a small lake formed by a dam on the river but the water, which was very calm, was emerald green.

The Driver stretched out on the embankment near a tight clump of birch trees, while Marie sat at the table to write postcards. Gradually some black clouds gathered above them and a breeze that heralded rain made the leaves of the birches and the surface of the lake shiver.

But the rain held off until they were back on the road. It began violently, with lightning and fierce thunderclaps, as they were driving through the village of Grande-Vallée. It rained so hard that even with the windshield wipers at top speed the Driver couldn't see fifty meters ahead. As soon as they spotted a road on the right they turned onto it with all their lights on, then immediately stopped on the shoulder.

The storm was over as abruptly as it had begun, and a gap in the clouds revealed a dazzling sun. Throwing the rear doors wide open they got out, hoping to see a rainbow. There wasn't one but the light was gleaming on everything they could see around them: the trees dripping rain, the water streaming off the road and an old wooden covered bridge straddling a river.

They walked on to look at the bridge. All at once, a backfiring motorcycle with a sidecar emerged, going flat out, forcing them to the side of the road; they had time to spot a big dog in the sidecar. When the bike was level with the bookmobile it suddenly slowed down and came to a stop a short distance away.

The driver dismounted. Tall and thin, with narrow shoulders, he was dressed in black leather from head to toe and his jacket was adorned with stars and polished stones and a metal chain. Strands of fair hair escaped from his full-face helmet and drifted carelessly on his neck.

When he took off the helmet, fair wavy hair cascaded onto his shoulders: he was actually a girl, a very young girl. She placed her helmet on the seat of the bike and leaned across to the dog crouched in the sidecar, a huge St. Bernard. She murmured something, the dog blinked and obediently stayed put.

With her hands in her jacket pockets, she strode up to the book-mobile, her heels ringing out on the asphalt. She stared hard at Marie and the Driver and then, in a surprisingly deep voice, asked:

"Have you got any books?"

"Yes," said the Driver.

"Can I have one?"

"Of course."

The Gaspé wasn't part of his territory, but faithful to his principle of never refusing anyone a book, he lowered the step and invited the young girl to climb in. He wasn't surprised when she stayed outside, merely glancing at the books: for some readers the library was a kind of sanctuary and you had to give them time.

Marie asked: "What's your dog's name?"

"Buddha," said the girl.

"Doesn't he get out of the sidecar?"

"That's for him to decide."

"Can I pet him?"

The girl looked her up and down, then turned towards the sidecar and produced an odd two-note whistle. The dog pricked up his ears.

"Okay," she said. "Go ahead."

Seeing that things were under control, she turned back to the bookmobile. She looked at the children's books that were fitted into the back doors, those for the youngest on the bottom shelves, those for the older ones above them. Then she stuck her head inside, but still didn't go in.

"Would you like a drink of something?" asked the Driver.

"Maybe," she said.

"Coffee? Hot chocolate? Coke?"

She shook her head, making her blonde hair dance on her leather jacket.

"Coke," she decided.

"What about your dog, is he thirsty?"

"Could be."

A brief and imperious whistle brought the St. Bernard lumbering out of the sidecar and up to the bookmobile. Marie came with him.

The Driver got into the van, opened a bottle of Coke and gave it to the girl. Then he poured water into a big soup bowl and held it out to Marie, who set it down in front of the dog. Very noisily, it began to drink.

The Driver got out and with a questioning look to Marie said: "We'll leave you for a while, we're going for a walk. You'll be more comfortable choosing your books."

"You don't have to," she said. "I'm not sure you've got the one I'm looking for."

"Is it a special book?"

"Yes."

"What kind?"

"A book that answers questions."

The Driver and Marie exchanged a look of concern.

"What questions?" he asked, his voice filled with doubt.

"Why we live, why we die. Questions like that."

He had read quite a few books in his life and the bookmobile contained a certain number, but he couldn't recall a single one that would give a satisfactory answer to her questions.

"We don't have what you're looking for," he said with a heavy heart.

The young girl didn't reply. She finished her Coca-Cola and walked back to her bike with her dog.

"I'm sorry," said the Driver.

She stepped on the starter pedal and kicked the bike into action. She lifted her hair off the back of her neck, pulled on the full-face helmet that was as black as the rest of her outfit, and got back on the road with the dog in the sidecar.

All day they were obsessed by a sense of failure, the impression that they hadn't done all they should have. That evening when they settled in for the night in a parking lot in a village whose name they hadn't even noticed, Marie lay down beside him on the folding bed. She curled up and soon they fell asleep, nearly clutching one another.

GANNETS

HE WAS the first to open his eyes. Surprised to see Marie's face so close to his, he brought his head back reflexively and that movement woke her up.

"Bonjour!" she said. "Did I keep you awake?"

"Not at all," he said. "Bonjour!"

He moved closer, his mouth shut, and rubbed his nose against hers.

"How about you?" he asked. "Did you sleep well?"

"Not really. I dreamed a lot but I've forgotten them, all except one: I dreamed that I had a baby. I used to have that dream often but the baby was always my mother's . . . This time it was mine."

She had a hint of a smile that put little lines around her mouth and eyes. Leaning across, he pulled the blanket up to her chin, taking care to cover her shoulders because it was chilly in the van.

"I had a dream too," he said, propping himself on an elbow. "There was a man dressed in black, some kind of inspector, who'd come to see the books. I opened the two back doors for him but there was nothing left inside the bookmobile: the shelves were empty."

He lay down on his back and observed the light slanting in through the skylight above their heads.

"It's sunny out," he said. "Chances are we'll get to Percé early enough to see the gannets."

"On Bonaventure Island?"

"Yes."

"Is today Saturday?"

"Yes. You're thinking about your plane?"

"No. I was thinking about my friends on the North Shore. Isn't it tomorrow night that they'll be back in Havre-Saint-Pierre?"

The Driver counted quickly on his fingers.

"That's right," he said. "Are you going to phone them?"

"Yes, but since they'll get there late the company office is liable to be closed."

"Maybe, but I've got the number of the *Roi de la patate* too. He's always there when the boat comes in . . . Don't worry."

"Thank you. What time is it?"

"Eight. We can loaf around for a while."

"We're in luck."

She yawned and stretched. He gazed for a moment at her face, which was both angular and soft, then he asked:

"Will you let me put my arms around you?"

She smiled by way of response and he put one arm under her head and the other around her waist, and he held her gently against him, stroking her back under the T-shirt. Then he began to plant little kisses on her face, as if he were tasting something; he lingered longest on her cheekbones. She let him, shy but obviously content: you could tell from the light that filtered through her half-closed eyes.

Suddenly, very near by, they heard a cat meow. They stayed there, motionless, holding one another, their knees entangled. The cat meowed again, but they didn't move. The third time, the Driver said: "Okay, he wants some milk . . . I'll go."

"No," she said, "I will."

They got up at the same time and got dressed. In any case, they would have to fold the bed into the wall to get access to the kitchen nook and the fridge. After everything was put away they opened the back doors and tiptoed out.

A big grey tomcat was crouching under the vehicle. He had a torn ear and a gash slanting across his muzzle.

"You've been in a fight? Life's been rough?" asked the Driver. He tried to approach with his hand extended, but the cat began to growl, fur bristling, ears flattened. "I understand," he said, "you're thirsty but you don't want anyone to get too close."

Marie went to get a bowl of milk. She set it on the ground, two meters away from the cat, and they walked off to let him drink in peace. At the entrance to the parking lot, a sign on a telephone pole informed them that they were in the village of L'Échouerie.

The tomcat drank a second bowl of milk, cleaned his whiskers and walked away, rolling his shoulders. After that they had a quiet breakfast of cereal, toast, and coffee, then Marie got behind the wheel. The road was steep now; the bookmobile climbed up slopes, rounded capes, and hurtled down hills, carried along by its weight. Fortunately, Marie knew how to downshift on the curves, then accelerate to straighten out the van. She slowed down when they got to villages, which appeared without warning, huddled deep in a bay, often at the mouth of a river.

It was starting to drizzle when they arrived at the tip of the Gaspé Peninsula, at Cap-des-Rosiers — the place where the coast of Quebec was closest to that of France. With the bad weather they didn't stop and were in Percé by noon. This time they went to a campground, where they would be more comfortable. The fine weather was already back. Leaving the van in the spot they'd been assigned on the flank of a hill, they walked into town, bought sandwiches and mineral water, and at the wharf alongside the Reception Center got into the first boat that was leaving for Bonaventure Island.

Halfway there they spotted a whale in the distance; it was so small they'd have mistaken it for a dolphin if another passenger hadn't identified it as a fin whale. When the little boat landed at the island they let the other tourists pass them, then started off on the shortest of the three or four trails that had been recommended. There was a pleasant mixture of shade and sunlight and Marie took pleasure in naming all the flowers she was familiar with. The walking wasn't difficult but the path kept climbing, so after twenty minutes they sat on a bench to catch their breath a little and eat their sandwiches.

Further along the slope was less steep and eventually they arrived at the gannet colony. Between the edge of the cliff and a wooden fence, in a moving, chirping mass, were congregated several thousand birds, their white heads capped in yellow; their bills were pointed towards their fellows who were circling above them, returning from the dark blue sea where they'd been diving for fish.

The noise and the smell were overpowering. The Driver and Marie decided not to stay any longer and got back on the path somewhat shaken, holding hands.

"Are you disappointed?" he asked.

"Not at all," she said. "I'm impressed and I've seen all kinds of interesting things."

"Such as?"

"A double-crested cormorant . . . a murre and a guillemot . . . And I heard the grumbling of a puffin but I didn't see it."

"All I saw was a bunch of birds making noise," he said ashamedly.

She squeezed his hand very hard.

"It takes patience," she said.

When they got to the bottom of the path there was no boat at the pier. To pass the time she pointed out the maneuvers of some gulls that were flying back and forth above the shore: they picked up sea urchins in their bills and dropped them onto the rocks to break the shells.

After a fifteen-minute wait, a boat came to pick them up and they went back to the campground in Percé. Contrary to their usual practice they ate in a restaurant that night, took a long walk, and went into some stores; Marie bought herself a blue sweater with a hood. They took boundless pleasure in doing little things together.

Inside the van the air was cool and damp, so they burned some alcohol and made hot chocolate. Again, they drank their chocolate sitting on the floor, facing one another and with their backs against the shelves of books. In the course of the evening they told each other things they remembered. The Driver recounted how at the very beginning, his father, without putting anything on paper, had come up with the design for converting the milk wagon into an unusual bookmobile . . . How, the first time he'd parked on a wharf, he had worried that no one would come . . . How he'd got the idea of forming networks of readers . . . How, in time, he'd given up library cards and any other formality.

For the pleasure of finding things they shared, they talked about their favorite books. When they began to feel sleepy they set up the two beds, but Marie got into the Driver's. Even though it wasn't really made for two people, they weren't too cramped. Once they were under the covers they helped one another undress.

"Are you cold?" he asked.

"A little," she said in her husky voice.

"I'll warm you."

He lay on top of her, trying to cover her entire body, even her legs; the two of them were the same height. She turned her head a little and he rested his cheek against hers.

Suddenly, he began to laugh softly.

"I thought of a story," he said.

"What kind of story?"

"There's a scene you often see in movies and it makes me laugh every time . . . A man and a woman are in love, they throw themselves at one another, they embrace and tear off their clothes, they drop onto a bed, they bite and scratch and pant, it's like a battle . . ."

"I don't want to fight with you," she said.

"Me neither," he said, letting himself slip to her side.

"But I feel so good in your arms."

"Really?"

"Of course."

"I'm afraid I'd displease you and I'd like there to be a kind of . . ."

"You please me a lot."

She smiled. By the wavering light from the alcohol flame he could see the little lines around her eyes. He started again: "I'd like there to be a kind of equality in . . ."

Suddenly, the flame went out.

"I'll go," he said. Lifting his side of the covers he got up, and groping in the dark, managed to find the alcohol and the matches. When he felt that the tin had cooled down enough, he filled it with alcohol again and struck a match; as it caught fire, the alcohol made a muffled sound. With his nudity lit by the new flame, he came back to bed where Marie, buried under the covers, declared:

"You're very handsome."

"No I'm not," he said. "I'm old and my skin is getting wrinkled all over."

"Like me."

"We're the same . . . It's strange that we both came such a long way before we met."

He shivered. She lifted the covers and he got in beside her.

"We still have a little way to go," she said.

"Yes," he said. "Shall we try to do that?"

"I want to very much."

"You're shivering . . ."

"It's nothing. I'm sensitive to the cold."

Now she lay stretched out on top of him. While she was warming him, he slowly caressed her back and hips, then he stopped with his hands linked behind her back and they stayed like that for a moment, not moving.

"Am I crushing you?"

"Hardly. You don't weigh much."

"Fifty-two kilos."

"Aha! I'm two kilos heavier!"

"I think I'm too thin. I don't think I've ever seduced a single person in my life. I'd need more curves."

"Women aren't supposed to seduce," he said.

"What are they supposed to do?"

"The same thing as us: try to make the world a little more livable . . . No, stay like that. I think you're perfect. You're perfect for me. Besides, there's a little corner of you I particularly like, just here . . ."

Gently, he toppled her onto her side and pressed his lips to the hollow between her neck and her shoulder. She made a kind of purring sound. Moving very slowly, he kissed her and caressed her neck and her breasts. She returned every one of his caresses and in small steps, taking very good care of one another, they slipped onto the slope of pleasure with the sweetest of sensual delights and under the protection of all the love stories that surrounded them.

THE FOSSILS OF MIGUASHA

THE FOLLOWING DAY was Sunday. Now Marie would be able to join her friends who were coming back to Havre-Saint-Pierre on the *Nordik Express*.

They dawdled in bed, partly to extend the pleasure of sharing the same warmth, partly because they were tired. But by late that morning they were once again gripped by the fear of arriving late in Quebec City. So they got up quickly and had a bite to eat and then, without even shaving, the Driver got behind the wheel. After a few kilometers, though, Marie took out the map and estimated how far they were from their destination. Actually they weren't late, they were slightly ahead of time and could even treat themselves to a stop at L'Anse-à-Beaufils, where she wanted to look for agates.

When they got to the village they left the bookmobile at the water's edge. A stroller instructed them that until they'd been polished by experts again and again, agates looked like any of the colored pebbles strewn along the beach. Half an hour later, they'd found a large number of brightly colored stones but they couldn't tell if they were genuine agates. Somewhat perplexed, they put the stones in the glove compartment with the road-maps, leaflets, flashlight, the notebook for the readers' networks, and the open box of LU cookies, then they got back on the road.

Around six p.m. they stopped at Miguasha, on the Baie des Chaleurs. They were very weary and the Driver's back ached. Miguasha was famous for its fossils of fish three hundred and fifty million years old. The building that housed the exhibition hall was closed, but by chance there was a pay phone outside.

The weather had turned as hot as midsummer again so they drove across a meadow and parked under the trees, at the edge of a cliff. Bringing the wine and the chicken sandwiches they'd brought in Carleton, they descended a long wooden staircase that took them to the shore. They ran into tourists studying rock fragments and others sticking close to the cliff, looking for fossils: maybe it was here that the famous *Eusthenopteron foordi*, a fossil of a fish considered to be the ancestor of amphibians, had been found.

Despite their fatigue, they walked to the first cove to get away from the tourists and sat on the sand. The chicken sandwiches were tasteless but the wine was very good: a Côtes-du-Rhône chosen to please Marie. They drank the whole bottle . . . Later, the Driver felt a hand on his shoulder. He woke with a start.

"What is it?" he asked, worried when he saw that it was dark.

"It's all right," said Marie. "It's nearly time to phone."

"It is?"

"It's ten-fifteen."

"We'd better hurry."

By the light of the moon, which was nearly full, they gathered up the papers, the remains of their sandwiches and the empty bottle, and hurried up the wooden stairs. After stopping at their vehicle to get the flashlight and the coins they'd accumulated with the long-distance call in mind, they went to the pay phone.

The Driver waited till it was exactly half-past ten, as if the boat schedules were accurate to the minute, and dialed the company's number. In the office, a man's voice told him that the *Nordik Express* had berthed a while ago. He asked for Slim, adding that he was a well-known acrobat. The man asked him to wait a moment. A minute or two later, Slim came on the phone. The Driver passed it to Marie and walked away a few steps.

From Marie's quavery voice, he realized that something abnormal had happened. She was asking question after question, she wanted to know where and when and why. It took her a while to calm down. Finally, after proffering all kinds of advice, she hung up.

There had been an accident at Natashquan. The band had performed before the people who'd come to watch the boat pull in and Slim had set up his wire on the wharf. Judging that the spectators weren't reacting enthusiastically, he had put the wire a little higher than usual. And he'd fallen, breaking his wrist.

They crossed the moonlit meadow in silence and went back to the van. The Driver switched on the night-light.

"Would you like a hot chocolate before we go to sleep?" he asked, in a hushed tone so he wouldn't disturb her thoughts.

"No thanks," she said.

"It'll do you good . . . Anyway, I'm making one for myself."

"All right."

He boiled water and fixed the two cups of chocolate. The wonderful old photo of Shakespeare and Company above the sink didn't have its usual radiance.

Marie drank without a word, staring into space. Her face was a little strained and it was obvious that she was worried sick. Out of respect, the Driver refrained from asking questions. When she'd drained her cup he took it from her and, bending over, kissed her forehead.

After waiting in vain for her to say something, he set up the bed, switched off the night-light, and got undressed. As the night was cleared he opened the skylight partway. Marie still hadn't moved; her mind was elsewhere. He helped her undress. Taking her hand he brought her to the bed and made her lie down under the covers besides him.

Moving closer to him, she murmured something that he only half heard.

"Sorry?" he said.

"It's my fault," she said. "I should never have left them alone. Slim's like a child, he needs to be the star. He wants to impress people and sometimes he goes too far. Someone has to keep an eye on him."

"Mélodie's there," he said softly.

"That's true. She's great, Mélodie. She can do so many things and she's funny and touching besides. I'm very fond of her."

"Maybe it was one of those accidents . . . the kind that happen by chance and that nobody can prevent."

"You're right. My head's not working properly. As usual, I'm being a mother hen and I feel guilty."

Sighing, Marie put her head on the Driver's shoulder. For a long time she didn't move. Her breathing became more regular and he thought she was falling asleep. Then she asked abruptly: "What about you, how is your head working?"

"There are two things going on. The first is that I feel old and tired tonight, like an old fossil."

"Me too. And the second?"

"The second thing," he said, hesitating, "is about what I mentioned the other day . . . our golden years and all that . . . Right now, I can't tell the difference between what's true and what's false. I'm a little lost. And I don't really feel like talking about it, I think all I feel like doing is sleeping."

"Let's try to sleep then. Maybe things will be clearer tomorrow."

He agreed, but before giving in to sleep he asked: "Tomorrow

· 189 ·

night we'll probably be in Quebec City . . . And your plane leaves two days later, right?"

"Yes," she said. "But I'm not too sure I feel like leaving."

"Oh no?"

"No. I feel a little lost too."

A ray of light came in through the skylight and he could see that she was smiling sadly.

"We're both tired," he said. "We have to sleep."

"Yes," she said. "Do you want me to set up my little bed so you'll be more comfortable?"

"No. Stay with me, please."

"All right."

"Before we go to sleep, will you come into my arms?" he asked. Then he shook his head and added: "I always say *my* arms . . . But actually I'm in your arms as much as you're in mine!"

"The main thing is that it's good for both of us," she said.

She raised her head and he slipped his left arm under her neck, the right one around her waist: they already had their little ways. Entwined like this, they kissed for a moment and took turns caressing one another but soon fatigue won out and they fell into a deep sleep.

In the middle of the night he woke suddenly and saw that she had turned her back to him. He went back to sleep and when he woke up again at dawn, she had turned to face him and was fast asleep.

THE BRIDGE TO
THE ÎLE D'ORLÉANS

AFTER DRIVING through the Matapedia Valley, whose most secret landscapes were in tune with their feelings, they could see the grandeur of the St. Lawrence again at Mont-Joli. They drove for a while longer, then stopped at the park in Le Bic to eat and rest.

After driving for four hours they arrived in Quebec City. The Driver parked in the laneway that ran behind the buildings on rue Terrasse-Dufferin. They took most of the baggage and went up to the fifth floor. The apartment, three modest rooms, seemed vast and luxurious to them.

They spoke very little, absorbed in the worries that came between them and at the same time brought them closer together. While Marie was taking a shower, he tidied up a little and listened to his phone messages . . . His sister Julie was about to start a new school year, her family was well and the bridge to the island was as beautiful as ever . . . Jack was up to his neck in his new novel and wanted his friends to know that he'd be turned into a recluse and that his wife was well . . . At the Ministry, they'd already received some of the books that had been borrowed during the summer tour.

All he found in the fridge was half a lemon, a container of yoghurt, and a saucer with a slab of butter smeared with strawberry jam.

Barefoot and wearing a white T-shirt, Marie was drying her hair with a towel when he came back. She took the big bag of groceries from him and offered to fix something to eat and set the table while he showered.

After his shower he put on his terrycloth bathrobe which always had some old Kleenex in the pockets and they sat across from one another at the table. She'd made real coffee and there was ham, liver, pâté, tomatoes, and a salad, with chocolate éclairs for dessert. As the table wasn't big enough for two their bare feet touched; Marie's were a little cold so he took them between his and rubbed them warm.

When they'd finished eating, they went outside while it was still light. These were the last hot days of summer. Many people were out strolling on the boards of the Terrasse and their shadows were inordinately long.

They walked along the Château Frontenac and stopped a few meters past it, just across from the funicular, and leaned on the railing. It was the exact spot where they had first laid eyes on one another. On the vast bay in the middle of which was the tip of the Île d'Orleans with its delicate, elegant bridge, a little mist hovered just above the water.

The Driver came closer to Marie until he was touching her elbow.

"I've got something special to tell you," he murmured.

"I know," she said. "I guessed when I saw that we were stopping here."

"Actually, I want to ask you a question."

"A question?" she asked.

Her voice, husky as always, was barely audible. He sensed that her elbow was shaking and when he looked at her, he saw that her hands were trembling on the railing.

"Don't worry," he said at once. "I've decided to do the autumn round and I just wanted to ask you if . . . if you would come too."

She didn't answer right away. The light mist that was floating above the bay had suddenly filled her eyes. Wiping them with the back of her hand she asked: "For better or for worse?"

"That's right," he smiled.

"My answer is, I will," she said.

He drew a little closer to her again, pressing against her hip, and put his arm around her shoulder. Standing close, they gazed for a long time at the river without a word. Then he declared: "This is my favorite landscape in the world."

She nodded that she understood and added, "I'm starting to be fond of it too."

"Whenever I see it again," he said, "a sentence comes back to me . . ."

"What's that?" she asked calmly.

"Just this little sentence: 'I feel the outline of the bay in my heart.' I can't remember where I read it."

"I like that too," she said.

She repeated it in an undertone, listening to the resonance that the words stirred in her. While they were leaning on the railing, the sun set behind them and they were enveloped in the great shadow of Cap Diamant. All the light took shelter on the St. Lawrence River and before it disappeared, it stayed behind to caress the elegant structure of the bridge.